"PUT THAT BOTTLE DOWN AND COME ALONG. OR BE CARRIED OUT. I DON'T CARE WHICH, AND THAT'S A FACT."

Sharper shrugged. "Hey, partner, no trouble," he said easily, smiling. Then he threw the bottle right at Gorman's face.

The ball from Gorman's army rifle splintered the bar. Sharper hit the floor with his gun out. He fired six times.

Blood starting from the holes in his chest, Gorman staggered back. The Springfield dropped from his hand. He stood there glaring hate. Blood streaming, Gorman fumbled inside his shirt and brought out a broad-bladed knife. Teeth clenched, he forced himself out into the room.

"Go down!" Sharper howled. "Go down, damn you! *Go down!*"

THE NIGHT RIDERS

Keith Jarrod

A DELL BOOK

To Sir and Mrs. House

Published by
Dell Publishing Co., Inc.
1 Dag Hammarskjold Plaza
New York, New York 10017

Dell ® TM 681510, Dell Publishing Co., Inc.

ISBN: 0-440-16368-4

Reprinted by arrangement with Doubleday & Company, Inc.

Printed in the United States of America

First Dell printing—July 1980

THE
NIGHT
RIDERS

PROLOGUE

The silence at night in the San Rael range was usually sharp as the blade of a knife, with no slight sounds to dull its edge. The stamping and snorting of horses in the Comstock family's corral wasn't loud, but it was conspicuous as a trumpet fanfare just the same. Cursing silently, Luke Cranston pulled himself back from the edge of sleep.

Probably a coyote or bobcat, the old hired man thought as he got out of bed. Nobody else in the house seemed to have heard the commotion. His years in these mountains had made his hearing more acute than most. He struck a match to light a kerosene lamp.

He pulled on pants and boots and an old checkered flannel shirt. It was cold this time of night, in spring, but he wouldn't be out long. Just long enough to scare off whatever was bothering the horses. The glow from the lantern would suffice to run off any of the small, man-wary predators who lived in the area.

He let himself out the back door so as not to disturb the sleeping household by tromping across the floor in his heavy boots. A thought struck him: Why wasn't Duke, the family shepherd dog, barking fit to wake the countryside clear to Ranchos de Taos? He came softly around the corner of the adobe ranchhouse and found his answer.

Luke all but tripped over the still form of the animal. Its head had been smashed by a single heavy blow.

The hired man looked toward the corral. There were men there—men on horseback, men on foot slipping wraithlike among the nervous beasts in the log enclosure. Their heads appeared white and ghostly in the starlight. Luke peered at them in surprise.

Then he realized each man's head was covered with a white cloth hood. And that could mean but one thing.

"Night riders!" he yelled. "Wake up, ever'body! It's the night riders!"

His shout brought the attention of the masked intruders, who started shouting to each other in Spanish and accented English. One spurred his mount at the hired man. The kerosene lantern bounced and rolled, miraculously not spilling as Luke dropped it to make a grab for a shovel stuck in the earth nearby. He swung it as the man closed in on him. The shovel connected with a *thunk!* and the man went backward over the horse's croup flailing his arms.

Lights went on inside the house. Angry Spanish voices cursed Cranston. He stood his ground, brandishing his weapon defiantly. The light from the grounded lantern gave him a wild look. A pair of riders approached menacingly.

"Stand back!" a voice barked. *"Para!"* The horsemen stopped where they were. A lone figure, tall on a sleek-sided black horse, stepped his mount into the lamplight. Luke raised his shovel.

"Get on out of here," he snarled. "Go on, *git!*"

The big man raised his arm. Flame flashed orange and a thunderclap roar destroyed the last stubborn remnants of the mountain peace. Luke flew backward into a heap, the shovel leaping from his fingers like a living thing.

The killer swung off the horse with the beast sidestepping and rolling its firelit eyes in terror. He stuck his smoking long-barreled revolver in his belt and picked the lantern from the ground. Glass exploded as he threw it through the nearest window. The lamp burst on a wall with a flare like a false sunrise.

For a moment all was deadly, ominously still, with only the crackle of young flames to break the quiet. Then the gunman climbed into his saddle. "Let's go!" he shouted with a wave of his arm, and dug in his spurs. The black galloped into the inky oblivion of the surrounding pine forest. A raider dragged the corral gate open, and the hoofbeats of the Comstock horses followed the intruders into the night.

The house was truly afire now. The wood furnishings provided good fodder for the flames. A Winchester spoke belatedly from a corner of the house. The shots echoed futilely after the marauders.

Luke Cranston lay on his back, wide-open eyes not seeing the glittering splendor of constellations overhead. A trickle of blood, purple-black in the flickering glare, ran down his shirt and dripped onto the thirsty mountain soil.

CHAPTER ONE

The late afternoon of the mountains was not like the late afternoon of the desert below. In the high country the cool of evening set in early. It was late afternoon now, and the edge was long gone off the day's heat. Still, the five men on horseback gathered around the tall Ponderosa pine were sweating.

Standing by itself halfway down the flank of a ridge, the mighty pine was bare of branches for the first ten feet of its height. The lowest branches were thick, sturdy enough to bear a man's weight.

Very soon, now, one would be doing just that.

A rope was tied around the bole of the tree and looped over the thickest branch. The other end was knotted around a man's plump brown neck.

The man in the noose was the calmest of the five. His dark eyes were mild as he looked at his captors, arranged in a semicircle around the hanging tree. Their eyes were hot and angry above the handkerchiefs tied over their faces. Their voices were harsh.

"God damn you, I ain't gonna ask again!" shouted one. "Where's that murdering bastard Villareal hiding out?" For emphasis he prodded the captive in his ample belly with his rifle, an old Henry repeater.

The rope chafed the prisoner's neck and the pokes in the stomach hurt. But his face was impassive, his voice reasonable as he replied, "I have no idea where Noe Villareal is. I have not seen him for many months. And I do not believe he is a murderer."

"Aw, listen at that chilibelly," another rider said.

Unlike the rifleman and the captive, both in their middle years, this one was scarcely more than a boy. But the tone in his voice was as menacing as the other's rifle, and his pale blue eyes like the eyes of an animal. "We know Villareal murdered old Luke. And we're gonna find him if we got to stretch the neck of every Mexican nigger in the San Rael Mountains."

The prisoner said nothing. He peered intently at the lean youngster's face as if trying to make out the features masked by the bandanna. In reality he was trying to avoid calling attention to what he'd just seen.

The five were no longer alone on the slope.

The top of the ridge was thickly covered with trees, and from there the lone rider had emerged. The captive shifted his rump on the bare back of his horse as he continued to scrutinize the blue-eyed vigilante.

"We'll find out anyway," a third rider said, a stocky man with a sunburned neck. "Might as well tell us, save us all some trouble."

"I have nothing to tell you."

The rider on the hillside was coming nearer. The vigilantes were so intent on their prisoner they had no idea what was behind them. If only their attention could be held a few moments longer, the prisoner thought, there might still be a chance for survival.

The rangy rifleman snarled something that was lost in the folds of his kerchief. "Well, it's your funeral," he said more distinctly. "Jerry."

The fourth horseman looked at him. He was another youngster, but without the brash assurance of the pale-eyed youth. What the captive could see of his face looked scared. The boy's eyes flicked to the other youth, who nodded. The boy gulped, pulled off his hat, and leaned down to whip the prisoner's horse from beneath him.

Twenty feet behind him, the newcomer cocked his pistol.

The Colt's 1873 Model Army six-shooter made a

distinctive multiple click when cocked, and no man who'd lived west of the Mississippi very long would mistake it for any other sound in the world. The masked men froze, Jerry half out of his saddle. Slowly they turned their heads.

"Good afternoon," the newcomer said. The Colt was in his right hand. In his left was a double-barreled, sawed-off shotgun with both hammers drawn back. His face was clean-shaven, framed by long blond hair. A red mark, a birthmark or scar, curled around the outside of his left cheekbone. His voice was mild, almost conversational.

The chunky masked rider wrapped his fingers around the butt of his gun and pulled. His gun cleared leather but dropped from his hand as though hot as the shotgun roared like a mountain howitzer. The prisoner cried out. His horse reared and bolted out from under him. He grunted explosively as he hit the hard-packed *caliche*. Shredded by buckshot, fragments of rope and tree rained down on him.

His horse hightailed it down the valley to the echo of the gunshot. Without being asked, the thin man dropped his Henry to the ground. The others stayed frozen.

"Very good," nodded the newcomer. "And now the gun belts."

The vigilantes obeyed without hesitation. The unfired barrel of the shotgun was a compelling argument backed up by the rock-steady Colt. The intruder had shown cool nerve and long, sharp teeth.

At a gesture from the shotgun the men sidled their mounts away from the tree. The twin bores never wavered as the rider came off his gray mare and walked to where the bound man sat stunned on the ground. The Colt went into a pocket of the swallow-tailed blue greatcoat the newcomer was wearing and a knife appeared in its place. The blade sliced the ropes holding the dark man's wrists behind his back and went away.

"Do you know how to handle a rifle?" the youth asked, drawing the revolver from his pocket. The freed captive nodded, rising uncertainly to his feet. He rubbed his neck where the rope had chafed it. Then he retrieved the fallen Henry and aimed it at his former captors.

"You may leave," his savior told the masked quartet.

"You're makin' a mistake, mister," the rifleman said.

"It could be," the youth agreed. "Concern yourselves with your own mistakes. Circling and trying to come on me unawares would be one."

The riders exchanged uneasy glances. "You will ride down the valley together—and I may take it in mind to follow you under cover of the trees. Return for your weapons in the morning, if you wish. But until you are safe at home in bed tonight, take it for granted I am nearby with a bead drawn between your shoulder blades."

Four horses wheeled as one and took off at a stiff trot. Every rider's back was rigid with anticipation of the sledgehammer impact of a .45 ball. Once out of pistol shot the vigilantes spurred to a gallop.

The two remaining men watched the dust of the retreating horsemen recede till it rounded the bend in the valley. The youth swept back his coattails with the heel of his right hand and holstered the Colt, butt forward. He coughed once, spat on the ground, and gave a snort of laughter. Then he walked to his mare and began wrapping the shotgun in oil cloth. Though the other couldn't see it his hands were shaking.

"I am grateful to you, señor," said the brown-skinned man. "But those men could return at any minute."

The youth laughed again, knotting the roll of oilcloth behind the cantle of his saddle. "Not likely," he said.

He walked to the scatter of weapons on the ground. Stooping, he picked up the gun the stocky rider had tried to draw on him. "Interesting," he said, squinting at it in the failing light. "A Thunderer, a double action made by Colt. Billy the Kid used one, I've heard. And that museum piece you're holding is right out of the Civil War. A keepsake, no doubt. They'll be back, but not till morning."

He shrugged and thrust the pistol into its holster. "They fear," he said. "They would come back with friends, but they'll want to keep this secret. Four men yielding to one—it would look bad, no?"

He pointed with his chin at an ornate high-backed saddle lying nearby. "That saddle yours?"

"*Sí*. They wanted me on bareback, so I would slide off more easily."

"Should I chase your horse down? He's very handsome."

"No," the other said. He let the Henry fall and rubbed at a luxuriant black moustache with the back of his hand. "Santiago is a clever horse. He will go straight home. Elena—my daughter—she will worry when he returns without me."

"I see." Smiling, the blue-coated youth swung into his own saddle. "Get your saddle and climb aboard. We must not worry the mademoiselle, Mr.—"

"Gonzalez. Eulógio Gonzalez."

The younger man reached down. Gonzalez took his hand and swung up with the saddle awkwardly under one arm. "A pleasure to meet you," the young man said as Gonzalez settled in behind him. "Call me Random."

CHAPTER TWO

Evening settled in to stay. The last rays of the sun spilled over the ridge tops, dyeing the squat mud-colored walls of the house a pale-flame orange. The surrounding woods were shadowed and mysterious as the gray emerged into the clearing with her double load.

"My *hacienda*," Gonzalez said proudly. It was a low, square, sprawling adobe. The dark ends of beams protruded in a line just below the top of the wall.

Movement stirred in a darkened doorway. Random brought the mare to an abrupt halt. The barrel of a Winchester was sticking out of the shadows, aimed straight at his midriff.

"Elena! It's me, *hijita! Tu padre*," called Gonzalez from his perch behind his rescuer. A slender young woman stepped from the porch. She held the rifle steady.

"Elena!" Gonzalez repeated sharply. Random realized the shorter man was completely hidden behind him. Random was tall and slim, standing six feet and two inches in his bare feet, and the enormous blue flannel coat exaggerated his bulk. Gonzalez clambered off the horse. The girl's face lit up.

"*Papá!*" she cried. "I did not see you. What has happened? I was so worried when Santiago came home without you. I sent Joselito out to look for you."

Gonzalez glanced at Random. "I am safe now," he

said, "thanks to this young man. He saved my life. So it is impolite to point that rifle at him, *querida.*"

The girl's mouth fell open. The rifle dropped from her fingers as she threw herself at her father. Random winced as the gun bounced on the hard earth, but it failed to go off.

Random was amused at the lightning shift of the girl's character. Facing an intruder across the sights of a Winchester, she displayed the same calm nerve her father had in the face of death a short time earlier. But the instant she heard of his brush with death, she became a little girl running to her father to be comforted and reassured.

Looking embarrassed, Gonzalez disentangled himself from Elena's embrace. He stepped back and regarded her fondly. She was a head taller than he and as willowy as he was round. A spot of color touched her high cheekbones as she realized the way she'd let down her guard in front of a stranger.

"This is Señor Random," Gonzalez said. "Señor Random, may I present my daughter, Elena María Gonzalez y Saavedra."

The girl curtsied and held out a hand. Random stepped forward and took it in his hand. His hand was surprisingly rough and muscle-corded, more like a mule skinner's or a miner's than one belonging to a fresh-faced youngster. He bowed and kissed Elena's hand with a flourish of his battered felt hat. Straightening, he smiled at her. Her black eyes showed surprise—she had expected Random to shake her hand according to standard frontier usage.

"*Charmé,* ma'amselle," he said. "I am at your service."

"*Mi gusto,*" Elena replied, lowering her eyes. "I owe you the life of my father." Her English was good, somewhat more fluid than Random's in fact. It was cool and formal, though; she was being the perfect Spanish gentlewoman now despite her lapse of a minute ago.

The doorway led not into the house proper but instead to a tiny courtyard, flagged with red sandstone, except for an open patch by the wall reserved for a garden. A few colorful flowers unknown to Random were closing their petals against the approaching dark. Lugging his saddle, Gonzalez ushered Random across the *patio* and into the house with Elena coming after.

The walls were thick and strong. Random nodded as he passed through the door. The walls and indirect ingress made the household easy to defend against intrusion. He could appreciate such considerations.

Within was darkness. Random's eyes adjusted to the light of a neglected fire burning in the hearth to show him a small and cozy sitting room, the walls lined with shelves of books. A young man was standing up from a low white-washed adobe bench built out from the wall. Gonzalez saw him and frowned.

"Roberto came to call on me this afternoon," Elena said hastily.

"And Joselito left you by yourself?"

"Oh, Father," Elena said. "Roberto would never think of taking advantage of your absence." Random felt that was wise of Roberto. He himself would not think of taking advantage of the girl, comely as she was, without her prior consent in writing. She had too steady a hand with a rifle.

Roberto was glaring at the newcomer with open dislike. Gonzalez, accepting his daughter's explanation, introduced him to Random as Roberto Morales, son of a neighboring rancher. Random put out his hand.

The Mexican youth shook it gingerly, as if expecting to find a live scorpion concealed in the palm. Random could feel Roberto's jealousy at a stranger being in the same room with Elena. But there seemed to be something else, an animosity in look and handshake, that went beyond a lover's simple possessiveness.

A door opened at Random's back and a short Indian appeared, carrying Elena's rifle. His shoulders were massive, scarcely narrower than the doorway, and his face was like a weathered slab of sandstone. His manner seemed to indicate disapproval of the way the Winchester had been left carelessly on the ground, but one of the flagstones outside would have shown no less expression than his wide flat face.

"This is Joselito," Gonzalez told Random. "This young *hombre* saved my life today, Joselito."

Obsidian eyes took in the stranger. Random tried to guess the Indian's age, found he could not. Joselito could be forty or seventy. *Like the Sphinx,* Random thought: ageless and impassive. The man's hair was straight, black with no hint of gray, gathered at the nape of his neck in a queue tightly wrapped in red cloth. He gave a slight nod and passed soundlessly from the room.

"Joselito is a Pueblo Indian, from Jemez," Gonzalez said. "As a child he was captured by the Mimbreño Apaches of Mangas Coloradas and held as a slave. They cut out his tongue."

"I see," Random said. He was foreign to this land, but not to such grim details of life.

Gonzalez clapped him on the arm. "You have ridden far," he said. "Will you do me the honor of staying the night beneath my roof? Elena is an excellent cook."

Random hesitated. His expression was unreadable. He had borrowed trouble by rescuing the Mexican—more than Gonzalez could have realized. It would be a further risk to stay overnight at the man's house.

But it was late and he was hungry. It would be boorish to refuse, and that went against Random's grain. At any rate, he might learn something.

"I would be honored," he said. He stepped onto the hearthstones with his hands deep in the pockets of his greatcoat. The night chill was coming on. He filled his lungs with fire-warmed air, easing the chill-born pangs of the old wound in his chest.

At his back Roberto Morales was expostulating angrily in Spanish. Random did not know the language, but he caught the word *"gringo"* repeated several times. Señor Gonzalez interjected once or twice, and finally Elena cut the youth off with a spate of fluid syllàbles. Whatever she said took the wind out of Roberto's sails. Random turned from the fire to see him stalking toward the door.

"I must apologize for the poor manners of my neighbor's son," Gonzalez said when Roberto had gone. "He was—he does not . . ." His voice trailed off uncomfortably.

"Roberto does not like Anglos," Elena said. "He was offended that my father invited you to dinner. With him, pride comes before manners." Anger showed in her proud features. "I am very sorry."

Random accepted her apology with a smile and a nod. He still had the impression he'd missed something.

Dinner was steaming plates of food rich with spices and melted cheese. The spice caused Gonzalez and his daughter momentary alarm as their *norteamericano* guest tucked into his fare like a ravenous wolf. The virulent Chimayo *chiles* could send the uninitiated leaping through closed doors with such howls of anguish as to convince the neighbors for miles around that some poor devil was being tortured by Apaches.

As it happened, the food not only failed to faze the visitor, but met with his eager approval. After one bite his brow wrinkled thoughtfully and he asked what he had just bitten into, stabbing with his fork at a cornshuck-wrapped cylinder of corn meal. It was a *tamale,* Gonzalez informed him. Random remarked that it tasted just like *couscous,* of which neither Gonzalez nor Elena had ever heard, and went back to demolishing the contents of his earthenware plate.

As they ate, Señor Gonzalez told his daughter the

story of his rescue from the four masked bravos. He told the tale with a wealth of gesture, but he stuck to the facts.

His gratitude and respect for Random came through clearly. When he finished Elena looked at the stranger in a way Random was sure Roberto Morales would dislike. For his part, he sat quietly, awaiting the question he knew Señor Gonzalez wanted to ask but hadn't. On any frontier it was poor form to question a man too closely as to identity, motivations, and antecedents. And Gonzalez had no wish to offend a man to whom he owed his life.

Elena asked the question for him. "You are a very brave man, Señor Random," she said, "and my family is in your debt. But what made you confront those men? There were four of them, and their victim was just a . . . just a stranger to you."

"Their victim was just a Mexican," Random said quietly. "That's what you were going to say, wasn't it?" The girl dropped her eyes. "I take it white men aren't much given to helping brown ones in this country."

Her downtilted face flushed. Candlelight rounded and softened her lovely patrician features with gold light and shadows. "It was not always that way, señor," her father told him softly.

A corner of Random's mouth quirked up. "It was not a particularly brave thing to do," he said. "I had them, and they knew it. I despise jackals who ride about in packs wearing masks and pulling lone men down." He rested chin in hand and sipped from a steaming mug of coffee.

Her eyes met his. The stranger's eyes were very green and seemed to glow in the candlelight.

"Now I have a question. Why were the jackals after you? Is that a common pastime?"

"No, it is not common," Gonzalez said. "Or at least it has not been before. You heard what they were saying?"

"Some. A murder of a man called Luke. A man named Via-something they felt was responsible. They thought you knew where he was."

Gonzalez sighed. "There has been a killing, a murder. A man named Luke Cranston, who never harmed anyone, was shot down last week in the dead of night by—by masked jackals who ride in packs. These jackals are *nativos*. My people."

Random could feel his shame. A sidewise glance at Elena showed she shared her father's feelings. "They believed you knew something. Any reason they should?"

"In these days it seems the color of a man's skin is reason enough to suspect him of many things."

"I understand." Random rubbed his cheek. "Tell me of these night riders, if you please."

Gonzalez shot a glance at his daughter. "They are called *las gorras blancas*, señor," he told Random, "after the white hoods they wear. That is what the name means, the White Hoods. Their aim is to drive the Anglo settlers from San Rael. They claim the Anglos plan the same for us."

"Fascinating," Random said casually, trying to mask the eagerness he suddenly felt. He leaned back. "I'd like to hear the whole story."

"It is a long one," Gonzalez protested. "I would not wish to—"

"Please."

"Very well. Let us go into the *sala,* and I will tell you everything you wish to know."

They rose. Joselito, the mute Pueblo, materialized and began to clear away the dishes. Elena stayed behind to help as the men went into the sitting room. The fire, replenished by Joselito, burned brightly.

Random found a chair and sat. Gonzalez plumped himself in a chair across from him. He began.

For years the Mexicans, or natives, and the Anglo settlers had lived in harmony. There were actually two villages named San Rael: the older Mexican village to the north, that had sprung up centuries before around the Cristo Redentor mission, and the Anglo settlement to the southeast which had grown around McMurphey's Mercantile, a general store established in 1860. Random and Gonzalez had passed to the north of the Anglo town, which lay athwart the San Rael Trail.

The first bad feelings had begun last summer. A railroad company had been seeking to build a rail line through the pass in the San Rael Mountains that the Trail crossed. Some of the larger Anglo landowners, standing to make a huge profit on the land sale, jumped at the deal. But other Anglos refused to sell their homes to the railway, and all the *nativos* had steadfastly turned down any and all offers the company made.

The railroad could not build a line that contained large gaps where landowners had refused to sell, and it was not economical to detour around the holdouts. The deal was called off.

The ranchers who had lost potential profits were bitter. There was talk of driving the natives off their land. It had been done before; the depredations against Mexican-held lands in the 1870s, under the corrupt Santa Fe Ring that controlled much of the Territorial Government, had been a major scandal. At the time nothing was actually done, but many natives grew fearful of what the future might hold. Distrust arose where none had been.

Then a new factor entered in the form of one Noe Villareal. A San Rael *nativo* by birth, Villareal had left the county when he was nine, after his father died, his mother having died when he was born. No one knew for certain what became of him in the intervening years, though rumor had it he'd taken a hand in the troubles between Anglo and native in neighboring Mora County.

Mora, Random was intrigued to learn, was the birthplace of *las gorras blancas*.

Villareal was an imposing figure. Lean, tall for a *nativo*, with a vast bandit's moustache and two enormous Walker Colt cap-and-ball revolvers stuck through his sash, he was the picture of the swaggering Mexican gunslinger of his day.

But he was more than a simple gun tough. According to Gonzalez he was a religious man, never without the crucifix of Barcelona silver he wore on a chain about his neck, the last bequest of his dying father. And he claimed that he wished to avoid violence. He only wanted the natives to organize themselves into a Citizens' Protective Association of the sort that cattlemen frequently formed, to assure that their rights were upheld. When the Mexicans were divided and bickering among themselves—which was usually, according to Gonzalez—why, that was when they were easy pickings for the Anglo *zopilotes*, the vultures who waited to snatch their hands with greedy claws. Organize and they cannot touch you, proclaimed Villareal.

The Anglos hated him and the young *nativos*, already spoiling for a fight, resented his emphasis on peaceful means. But he was an incredibly forceful personality, a powerful and persuasive orator. Slowly, haltingly, the first steps toward forming the Association were taken.

No more than those first steps were ever taken. One day the Anglo sheriff and two hastily deputized assistants rode to the native village to arrest Villareal, on the strength of a telegram from the town marshal of Durango, Colorado, to the effect that Villareal was wanted for bank robbery and murder in that city.

Warned somehow, Villareal left town a few steps ahead of the sheriff. He had not been seen since.

Random was puzzled. "Those men mentioned Villareal," he said. "They claimed he murdered Luke Cranston. How is this possible, if he hasn't been seen since fall?"

"I should say, no one can say for certain he has

seen him," Gonzalez amended. "Many have seen a man they believe to be Noe Villareal."

A few weeks after Villareal's disappearance some of the younger *nativos* gathered by torchlight to hear a man speak. His face was obscured by a white hood with holes cut for the eyes. He was a tall, spare man whose Spanish was the Spanish of San Rael. And he told the young men what they wanted to hear.

Rise up! said the hooded man. *Ride against the* gringo *intruders! They seek to drive you from your lands, the lands that have been yours for generations. Let* them *be driven out instead!*

The young men listened. The young men responded. The night raids began.

They started as little more than pranks. Fences were cut, corrals pulled down, Anglo families living on isolated ranches were awakened in the small hours of the night by dreadful, if harmless, cacophonies of screams and shots fired into the air. Gradually, the raids grew more serious, as stock was run off and dogs killed.

Over the winter the attacks had continued in a steady trickle. The night riders were always careful to cover their tracks, and attempts to trail them invariably met with failure. Many head of cattle and a number of horses disappeared.

With the coming of spring thaw the tension increased. *El Jefe,* as the mysterious leader of the *gorras* had come to be called, claimed that the Anglos were planning to bring suit in the county court at Los Duranes to have the boundaries of *nativo*-owned land redetermined. When this had happened in other parts of the Territory, as his listeners well knew, it always resulted in the land in question diminishing in size, while that of neighboring *gringos* increased.

Was this to happen in San Rael?

Not while the *gorras blancas* rode!

The first houses burned. Families huddled beneath the stars and watched their lives crackle skyward in smoke and dancing flames, while the hooded raiders melted tracelessly into the night. Elusive as phantoms, the White Hoods struck and struck again.

Then, ten days ago, the raids claimed their first life. It was said that *El Jefe* himself had gunned down Luke Cranston—a harmless man who was known to be a good friend of the *nativos*. Now the two communities were divided into armed camps, each dreading the other.

A war waiting to happen.

"And *El Jefe* is Noe Villareal," Random said when his host finished.

Gonzalez shrugged. "As I told you, no one can say *for certain* that they have seen Villareal. *El Jefe* only showed himself at night, like a *brujo*, a sorcerer. He always wears the *gorra* over his face. But his form is much like Villareal's, and his speech, except that where Noe Villareal counseled peaceful action, this man calls for blood."

"Perhaps he was bitter at being forced to flee," Random suggested. "He may have thought he was being persecuted. But why the mask? Why not show himself openly?"

The portly native tugged at his moustache. His eyes were sad. "Who can say? We Spanish are a romantic people. The idea of a fugitive from *gringo* injustice, who must hide out by day and who conceals his identity when he rides out for vengeance at night—this appeals to the young *caballeros*."

Random sat back. He put back his head and stared at the heavy beams holding up the ceiling. "It seems to me this *Jefe* is the real force behind your night riders," he said at length. "You said the young men were looking for trouble before he came. But it took his leadership to bring about the raids. True?"

"That is true. Before it was all talk, no more. Why do you ask?"

"No reason. Curiosity." Random disliked the tack the conversation was taking. In fact he did have a reason, one which he did not care to confide to his host. He changed course as smoothly as he could. "You don't believe Villareal is *El Jefe*."

"No," said Gonzalez, surprised. "That is not his way. He did not want us to fight the Anglos. He knew we could only lose, as the *indios* have lost when they fought the Americans. And there is more. Last week an old man, Eloy Sálazar, was dragged from his home and beaten by the *gorras*. He had said we natives should help the Anglos round up the White Hoods and put them in prison." Gonzalez frowned. "Noe Villareal would not encourage our people to turn on each other."

It was Random's turn to shrug. "Still, he seems the most likely candidate."

"That is also true," Gonzalez said sorrowfully.

Alone in the *sala*, Random sat and read by the light of a kerosene lamp. The book was *Duran County Days*, by a Mrs. Penelope Vardeman, published in 1880 by a Santa Fe company. Mrs. Vardeman was the widow of Col. Robert E. Vardeman, one of the first white settlers to move into what would become Duran County after the signing of the Treaty of Guadalupe-Hidalgo in 1848. Though it had been published long before the coming of the *gorras* to San Rael, the book provided Random a good picture of what life was like in the Territory and Duran County. He was new to this land, and so the reading was worthwhile despite Mrs. Vardeman's effusive style.

Elena Gonzalez came into the room, graceful and silent. For a time she watched the strange young man who had saved her father's life. He spoke peculiarly, sometimes using words that were neither English nor Spanish, without seeming to realize that he did. Who was he? What was he? Where had he come from?

The girl's eyes went to the mark on his cheek. It looked like the curl of a question mark. It could have been an unusual birthmark, but to Elena it looked more like a brand.

Random looked up. His green eyes pinned her. An odd light seemed to flicker behind them, and a muscle twitched in his cheek, beneath the tiny brand.

It was as if he knew she was staring at his scar—she was suddenly sure it was that. She dropped her gaze, confused.

Random snapped the book shut and stood. When Elena looked back at his eyes the glint was gone and he smiled. "My thanks for the meal," he said. "I've not had better in a long time. Good night."

He replaced the book on its shelf. Then with a scrape and a thump of his boot heels he was gone to bed.

CHAPTER THREE

"Why should we let you make conditions?" demanded the red-faced man in the checkered vest. "Gunfighters are a dime a dozen in these parts."

"That may be," Random replied evenly, "but when you hired me you did not hire a gunfighter. A professional, yes. But of a different sort."

Daylight streamed in past frilly curtains. Random sipped his heavily sweetened tea and surveyed the faces of his would-be employers. They looked ill-assorted and out of place in the decorous sitting room of the big, white antebellum house.

When trouble threatened the white settlers of San Rael, these were the men who stepped forward to meet the crisis: Martin Stern, the town doctor; Lucius Tanner, rancher, big and rawboned with a steel-gray moustache; Henry Bacon, slight and sad-eyed, another rancher; Sheriff Hoopwright, chinless and balding, with big blinking eyes; Tag Carroll, the belligerent rancher in the checked vest; and finally, Clayton Barnes. Barnes was clearly the leader of the group, tall and lean and piercing of eye. He presided over the meeting from a plush chair, a glass of whiskey to fortify him against the pain that showed periodically on his face.

A month earlier, these six men had come to the decision that drastic measures needed to be taken against the night riders. The exact measures necessary were the subject of much debate. Tag Carroll had pointed out then, as now, that gunslingers were quite

easy to come by. There were even a few young men
in San Rael who would be willing to whip the *gorras
blancas* into submission.

The difficulty was that gunfighters had a poor
record in that line of work. The example of the
Maxwell Land Grant War was clear in everyone's
mind—bringing a celebrated bravo like Clay Allison
into the conflict had complicated matters and given
his employers very little satisfaction. Also, the Territorial Government was eager to avoid another land
war like the Maxwell or Lincoln County fights. If the
Anglos of San Rael began importing gunfighters by
the carload, the Governor was almost certain to send
in troops. And the Anglo ranchers suspected the cur-
rent Governor had a sneaking sympathy for the *nativos*.

It was Barnes, respected by white and native alike,
who provided a solution. An agent of his in St. Louis
had heard a man was putting out feelers to find work
as a professional soldier—a mercenary. Though he
was quite young and looked younger, his credentials
were impressive. In fact, Barnes had already heard of
the man. Here was the answer, Barnes told his com-
patriots. An ex-French Foreign Legionnaire and a
hero to boot, he should be just what they needed.

And so with fifty dollars' earnest money in the
pockets of his long *capote*, the swallow-tailed blue
coat of the Legion, Random had ridden west on his
gray roan mare. On the way, he had spent the night
in the house of a man whose life he had saved, a detail he had not mentioned to his employers. Nor did
he plan to.

After an uneasy night's sleep, Random had back-
tracked to where he and Gonzalez had left the San
Rael Trail. He was expected to ride in by that route,
and didn't see any point in having to explain why he
had come in from the direction of the Mexican village instead. The pile of weapons the vigilantes had
left behind the afternoon before had been duly col-

lected, whether by their owners or others Random
had no idea.

Having made some enemies already, Random followed the ridgeline overlooking the Trail till he came
to the valley where the Anglo settlement lay. No one
was likely to gun him down in plain view of town, he
decided. He returned to the Trail and descended
along it.

He was not worried that the story of his rescuing a
Mexican would have gotten around. No four men
would want it known far and wide that they had
been buffaloed by a lone rider. And if they had
wanted their names and faces to be connected with
their grisly errand, they would not have taken the
precaution of wearing masks. There would be no difficult questions about why a soldier of fortune hired by
the whites had saved the life of a native.

Still, Random would keep his back covered while
he was in San Rael.

If he'd taken a handful of adobe and wood structures and clumped them around a single mud street
flanked by a saloon, a general store, and a stable, he
would have had about all there was to San Rael, New
Mexico. Random guessed there was even less to the
nativo village. Probably a hundred souls lived in the
town proper. The rest of the whites were scattered
like windblown chaff over the hills on their isolated
ranches and farms.

It was a setup ideal for night-riding marauders.

The Barnes house had been a surprise. For one
thing, it was a mansion, not just a house. A lordly
frame building sitting on a hillside on the western
outskirts of San Rael, it presided over the valley like
a feudal baron. Lesser buildings huddled around the
great house like courtiers. Of the hundreds of head of
cattle Random had heard Clay Barnes owned, not
one was in evidence. Like the other big ranchers,
Barnes ran most of his stock on a high meadow south

of town, where the combined herds were tended by hired cowhands.

There was a massive brass knocker on the door. Random's echoing knock had been answered by a tiny Nego girl in a black-and-white maid's livery.

"Can I help you, suh?" the girl asked. Behind her Random saw a foyer carpeted in deep-pile burgundy. Expensive, patterned paper lined the walls. An enormous old painting of a Virginia fox hunt hung just beyond the maid's left shoulder. It was all straight out of the Deep South of 1847. In the New Mexico Territory in the Year of Grace 1883, an entire tribe of Bedouins, tents, camels, veiled women and all, would have looked no more alien.

Politely the girl repeated her question. Random handed her a card from somewhere within his greatcoat. She took it and had just turned away when someone came into the foyer behind her.

"Who is it, Lacey?" a voice enquired. The voice was young and feminine and very pretty, and so was its owner, when she stepped into Random's view, all daintiness and crinoline. Blonde and pink-cheeked, with eyes the color of the San Rael sky.

Random swept off his hat and bowed. "Good morning, mademoiselle," he said. "Is Mr. Clayton Barnes at home this morning?"

"Why, he surely is," the girl said, looking him over. He seemed to read approval in her face. "Come right on in and make yourself comfortable, Mister—?"

"Random."

"Oh, Mr. *Random*." Her eyes lit up. "Why, Lacey, run along right this minute and tell Uncle Clay that Mr. Random is here." The black maid relieved Random of his hat and coat and then disappeared up a flight of stairs to do her mistress' bidding. The hefty black Colt riding butt-first at Random's hip got no special attention from either female. Out here such particulars of attire were the rule rather than the exception.

"Whom have I the honor of addressing?" Random asked. His formality was as natural to him as the slightly hesitant manner of speaking, or the foreign words that occasionally slipped from his tongue.

The blonde girl was enchanted. "I'm Junella Barnes," she said, extending her hand. Random took it and kissed it as he had Elena Gonzalez', with a bow that would have done credit to an Austro-Hungarian diplomat.

"*Enchanté,* ma'amselle."

"Ooh," Junella said, blushing with fascination and delight. "*Très heureuse,* m'sieur. *Est-ce que vouis êtes Français?*"

"*Je suis Americain.*" Random laughed. "But almost a Frenchman, for the past five years."

"That sounds exciting." Junella ushered Random to the sitting room. It seemed crowded already, on account of the numerous portraits of Revolutionary War officers and their ladies. Barnes had apparently tried to transplant his whole Southern way of life when he moved to the less refined Territory. Random found it unsettling.

"Uncle Clay will be down to see you in just a minute, Mr. Random," Junella said. "You mustn't let him overexert himself, please. He had an accident several months ago—his horse spooked at a rattlesnake while he was out riding and threw him. It hurt his back very badly. The pain comes and goes— right now he's feeling all right, but the doctor says he'll have bad spells come on suddenly from time to time."

"I'll be careful," Random assured her. "You live here alone with your uncle?"

Junella sat in a plush chair embroidered with vines and flowers. "Please have a seat, Mr. Random," she said with a gracious wave of her hand. "He's not really my uncle—he's a distant cousin of some kind. My parents were killed twelve years ago. He's my guardian now."

"Another accident?"

She shook her head. "Comanche Indians. We lived in West Texas. I was born there."

The servant girl, Lacey, came down the stairs to announce Mr. Barnes would be down presently. Junella asked her guest's preference in refreshment, then sent Lacy to fetch tea for the both of them. "Unc—Mr. Barnes was my nearest living relation. He's a wonderful man, Mr. Random. Everyone thinks so highly of him. Even the Mexicans like him—he talks their language real well." Random noted that the idea of her Uncle Clay speaking "Mexican" seemed distasteful to the girl.

"He fixed this old place up the way it is now," the girl went on, brightening. "Said he'd make it a fit place for a young lady to be brought up in."

"I see." Random's eyes wandered. They fell on a table across the room. His brows went up.

"What do you see?" the girl asked. She looked at the table.

An open magazine lay on it. Reproduced on the page was a photograph, formally posed, of a young man in a military tunic. His expression was solemn, but the eyes above his bristling pale beard were bright, amused, self-mocking.

Junella leaned forward to pick the magazine up. "Uncle Clay left this here for me to look at," she said bemusedly. "I haven't—but wait. This is—"

"That's the issue of *Monde Illustré* for the week of July seventeenth, 1882," Random said, leaning back in his chair. "The picture is of Lieutenant Random, of the twenty-first demi-brigade of *La Légion Étrangère*."

"It *is* you. But the beard—"

"Went by the wayside, I'm afraid."

"It was half burned away in the North African desert," a voice said from the foyer. "A tribesman fired his musket into Mr. Random's face at point-blank range. The ball missed its target, fortunately. It's all in the article."

"The other half was shaved off by hospital orderlies," Random said, rising. "You are Mr. Clayton Barnes?"

"Call me Clay," the man said. He had come down the staircase whose bottom was out of sight in the foyer. Now he came into the sitting room extending his hand. Random stepped to meet him. Barnes's hair was gray, drifting to white at the temples. He walked with the aid of a cane, wincing once or twice, but otherwise he looked strong. His grip was firm and dry, and in his purple silk dressing gown and slippers he stood almost as tall as Random.

"I take it you've met my ward, Junella," he said as he seated himself with visible relief. Random nodded. "You ought to read about our young visitor's exploits, my dear. Quite fascinating. He was awarded the *Médaille Militaire* and promoted to captain for his bravery."

"The promotion part was a mistake," Random said, resuming his own chair. "They thought I was going to die on them, and the French love nothing better than a dead, decorated hero, especially a foreigner who's given his life for *La Belle France*. They felt captain was a more dashing rank than lieutenant. When I recovered they tried to set matters right by sending me to Indo-China to fight the Black Flags, but my doctors had told me to stay away from wet climates. So I took my discharge instead."

Barnes laughed. "I trust you find the climate here in the Territory amenable, sir?" Random made an easy gesture. "I have taken the liberty of inviting several other gentlemen here to speak with you. If you accept the commission they—we—will be your employers."

An hour later they were all there. After prospective employers and employee had sized one another up, they got down to particulars. Almost immediately they ran into a snag.

The youthful outsider made it clear he would only accept this job if his terms were met. From Tag Carroll's outburst Random knew the heavy-set rancher with the red face would be the one most opposed to the methods he used. Mr. Carroll, he guessed, favored going in and teaching the natives a "lesson," if not wiping them out for good and all. And every bit of Random's experience told him that would be just exactly the wrong thing to do.

"We've been through all this," Clay Barnes told Carroll soothingly.

"I know, I know," Carroll muttered, shaking his head like an angry bull. "But it grates on me just the same, the thought of white men antsing around with these Mexican niggers. Why don't we just ride on down to Mextown and burn 'em out? Man to man, a white can take a Mex any time."

Bull's-eye! Random thought. "Man to man is just the way you'd be fighting them," he said acidly, "and woman to woman, and child to child. I thought you wanted a stop put to these raids, not a war begun."

"Don't forget the Army, Tag," Dr. Stern said.

Random narrowed his eyes. He did not want the U. S. Army involved. He was sure it wouldn't look kindly on competition from free lances.

"I ain't about to," Carroll said. He turned to Random. "Mister, if us good white folks try to protect what's rightfully ours, you know what the yellow-bellied Territorial Government is gonna do? They'll scream for the Army, and we'll be knee deep in uppity nigger horse troopers from Fort Union. Prob'ly make us pull up stakes, give the whole shootin' match to them greasers."

"The Territorial Government is leery of siding with settlers in disputes with the natives," Barnes explained.

"Leery, hell. They've sold us out!"

"The last administration was tarnished by involvement in similar difficulties. You've heard perhaps of the Santa Fe Ring, Mr. Random? No matter." Barnes spread his hands wearily. "Gentlemen, I thought we had agreed upon a course of action. Shall we carry through with it, or go on arguing?"

"Let's get the hell on with it," said the rancher named Tanner, the tall one with the impressive gun-metal moustache. "Something has to be done. If this don't work we can try something else."

"You've nothing to lose by trying it my way," Random put in. "If I fail, I don't get paid. You're out nothing. If you could handle the problem without outside help you would have done so. And even if you trusted the Army, where would it get you? In the St. Louis papers I read of a young Chiricahua Apache who is cutting a bloody swath through the Arizona Territory, Army, settlers, and all. At what cost, gentlemen? One Apache shot dead—by a bunch of miners. The Army couldn't help you if it wanted to."

"And you can?" Carroll asked.

"Yes."

"Talk's cheap, son," Tanner said. "How?"

"First, establish patrols to fend off any future raids."

"Can't be did. Ain't enough men," Hoopwright piped up, pleased to be able to contribute something. He had been sitting by looking uncomfortable, since it was his responsibility to keep the peace in San Rael—and this meeting had come about because the peace wasn't being kept. Now he tried to look authoritative. He might have made it if he'd had a little more in the way of a chin, Random mused.

"It will require very few men, Sheriff. In actuality there are only so many paths the raiders can take. Give me a map and some men who know the country, and we can seal them all."

"You can't fight a war with maps," Carroll scoffed.

"You can't?" Random said mildly. "I've seen more men die from not being able to read maps—or not bothering to—than just about any other brand of stupidity."

"He's right, Tag," Barnes said. "We should have thought of it before."

"Does sound good," Bacon offered, almost timidly. Besides the sad-looking eyes he had a seal-colored moustache, as droopy as Tanner's was fierce. He looked like a basset hound. "But what next?"

Random took another sip from his tea. He didn't want to display too much foreknowledge of the situation. His dealings with Gonzalez were harmless—in fact, he thought they could be turned to his, and his employers', advantage—but it would be hard to convince these suspicious, anxious men of that. And there was only so much he could pretend to have learned from Barnes's agent in St. Louis.

"Do you have any idea who leads the *gorras blancas*?" Random asked.

The townsmen eyed each other. "Nobody knows for sure who he is," Tanner said at length. "Not even the Mexes. Word is, he ain't never seen without that white hood they all wear. And he only comes out at night. But we do have us an idea who he *might* be."

"Bullshit," snorted Carroll. "You know as well as I do, Lucius. A stinking, troublemaking greaser bandit named Noe Villareal."

Random made himself raise an eyebrow as if hearing the name for the first time. "Señor Villareal was very active here last summer," Clay Barnes said. "He was trying to organize the natives. He seemed to be a good man, though a bit extreme." Carroll snorted. Random recalled that Junella had indicated her guardian felt sympathy with the *nativos*. It was a factor on Random's side. He had a feeling he'd need something to counterbalance the fire-breathing Tag Carroll.

"However," the gaunt landowner continued, "he

did leave town in something of a hurry last fall."

"Got a telegram from Durango," Hoopwright volunteered. "Said he was wanted for sticking up a bank and gunning down a clerk. Went looking for him and he lit out like a jackrabbit for the hills. Ain't been seen since."

"It's Villareal behind them raids, all right," Bacon said with surprising vehemence. "Always swaggering around with them two Walkers stuck through his belt. Typical God damn Mex shootist."

"Bastard shot Luke Cranston, same as he did that teller," Carroll said. "I allus said we should have strung him up when he first came around, stirring up the chilibellies."

"If Villareal is the leader of the *gorras*," Dr. Stern's quiet voice cut across the others', "then what do you propose to do about it, Mr. Random?"

"That much is simple," Random said. "Kill him."

CHAPTER FOUR

Afternoon breezes plucked at the map. Random bit his lip and shifted his hold on the unwieldy sheet of paper. He peered from it to the landscape, then licked the tip of his pencil and made a notation.

To the northwest were two snow-capped peaks, blue and white in the distance. They had served as landmarks to guide him to the troubled town of San Rael. *Las Hermanas* they were called, the Sisters. They dominated the San Rael range through which the pass ran from the eastern plains to the Rio Grande Valley. The Trail went through that pass, and so did the proposed route of a rail line.

North of San Rael lay a tortuous tangle of hog's-back ridges, hills, and arroyos, covered with junipers and scrubby *piñones*. The higher elevations were forested with tall Ponderosa pines. To the south was the high meadow, clear-cut back in '65 and grazing land ever since. There the Anglo stockowners ran their cattle under the watchful eyes of their cowboys.

To Random, this meant that his southern flank was safe. The wide-open meadows would offer no cover from the rustler-wary wranglers. *El Jefe* had shown himself to be as clever as an old dog *coyote*. He would waste neither time nor men trying to attack from the south.

Likewise, Random felt there would be no raids coming from the west, straight up the Trail, which was fairly broad and tended to carry traffic at odd times. The Trail would be an ideal route for a large, slow-moving army. But it was too exposed and inse-cure for the white-hooded raiders.

That left the north and eastern sides of San Rael. The young mercenary steadied the map against a shift in the wind that slapped his long coattails against his stirrup flaps. He had spent an hour with Tanner and Hoopwright fixing the location of the raided homesteads on the map, and it had paid off. Without exception, the *gorras'* victims lived to the east or north of the Anglo community.

Back in Sheriff Hoopwright's office—in a corner of an old hide warehouse, the original town jail having been burned accidentally during the Centennial celebrations back in 1876 and never rebuilt—Random had sketched in a few possible routes for raiding par-ties to take from the Mexican village. The map was a good one, a product of the recently completed con-tinental survey the U. S. Geological Service had car-ried out, finely detailed and, from Random's own reconnaissance, accurate.

Tanner and the sheriff both had been skeptical of the value of this preliminary paperwork. Random had explained the situation as he saw it to them. A leader operating at night with untrained men would not want to split his parties up. If separated, some of the raiders could get lost, or groups of them could blunder into each other, panic, and open fire. Even in the Legion, men were often lost to friendly fire be-cause of mistaken identity in the dark. Also, Random was certain it took the powerful personality of *El Jefe* himself, or a trusted lieutenant, to keep the raiding parties from dissolving back to the safe comfort of home and hearth.

So the *gorras* would leave the *nativo* settlement all in a bunch. And for groups of six to possibly twenty men, the estimate Barnes's St. Louis man had given Random, that meant they would need fairly clear trails. The routes Random outlined could carry the night riders to within half a mile of any of their former targets. Once they got that close, slipping up on the unsuspecting homes had proven easy.

Now Random sat astride his gray mare humming to himself with satisfaction. Practically at the mare's feet was the steep bank of an arroyo. And the sandy floor of the wash was churned by the hoofprints of numerous horses.

The arroyo was two miles from the nearest dwelling, Anglo or native. By following it east for five hundred yards, a person could climb the bank and come out of it on the far side of a low ridge from the Comstock ranch, the last site raided by the White Hoods. And by backtracking a ways, you found it fed into one of the two bigger washes Random had judged the *gorras* would use to leave their village.

There had been no rain to wash away the raiders' tracks since the Comstocks were hit and Luke Cranston killed.

It was a minor victory. Random now had proof his theories were right. And he felt sure that, as he'd said, a few men could contain the raids with ease. With such successes he could undermine Tag Carroll and however many of the townspeople supporting him, making it difficult for the red-faced rancher to stir up any of the kind of violent retribution he favored. Right now Carroll and the hotheads were a bigger danger than the *gorras,* because any violence from them against the Mexican community at large could spark a bloodbath.

Following the arroyo to where it joined the larger wash, Random found no more prints. He guessed that when possible, *El Jefe* ran his horses along the hard-packed rims of the arroyo, to leave as few tracks as he could.

The gray's big, speckled ears pricked up. Random heard sand crunching and came around a bend in the arroyo to be confronted with a herd of cows. Not a herd, precisely, but a knot of about ten skinny creatures, plodding along in the charge of a brown-faced boy of eight or thereabouts. Random smiled and waved, but the boy eyed him sullenly and remained silent.

Random rode back to where he'd seen the prints. They were unbroken half circles, not split like cows' hooves. Horses had definitely made them. He grinned ruefully.

Random wondered if the boy always took his beasts up that particular gulley, or if somebody had just suggested he do so for only a few days, *por favór?* It was a neat way of eradicating telltale hoofprints. Random was willing to bet the *gorras* would never be tracked, thanks to little boys with a few head of cattle to watch over. It had been a break to find such tracks as he had.

The shadows were beginning to grow longer when Random brought his mare down the long flank of the ridge overlooking the little town. Children played beside a house on the slope, smiling and waving to him as he passed. He could not help but contrast them in his mind with the solemn *nativo* boy.

It was time to meet with the men Tanner and Bacon had gathered to serve as his patrol. Random was due to meet with them at the clapboard schoolhouse, which stood by itself across the road from the Barnes mansion. He had picked the school as a headquarters because it was in a central location but out of the town proper. Random didn't want outraged townspeople swarming out to meet the next raid, whenever it came. Men could slip in and out of the schoolhouse without alerting the whole valley.

On the main thoroughfare of San Rael, the first person Random encountered was little Henry Bacon, just coming out of the sheriff's office. The corners of Bacon's moustache twitched up in a smile of greeting and he swung up onto his fine chestnut gelding, nudging the beast into step beside the young mercenary's gray roan.

"Got fifteen, sixteen men down at the schoolhouse for you, Mr. Random," he said. "Good men."

"Any of them victims of the *gorras*?"

"Nope, not a one, just like you asked." He shot a puzzled look at Random. "Mr. Carroll was mighty upset over that. Said the ones the Mexes hurt were the ones we should use. Give 'em a chance to get their own back."

"They are the ones we do not want," Random said stiffly. "A man out for vengeance is fast on the trigger. He starts seeing red and shoots without thinking. We can't afford—what's this?"

They were passing the mudwalled *cantina*. Two men had just come out of the double doors and were blinking into the unaccustomed glare. One of them was Carroll, his familiar reddish cast deepened by a few shots of rotgut whiskey. With him was a black-haired boy of maybe nineteen, who wore a pair of sixguns low and had that manner that proclaims to man and beast that the bearer is bad, bad news. He looked like the kind of tough, heartless kid who'd pump Colt lead into a man for the pleasure of watching him writhe.

But it wasn't the kid's affected desperado manner that made Random stiffen and stare through slitted eyes. The face he'd never seen, but the lean, muscular figure was familiar. So was the fidgety white-stockinged black stallion tethered next to Carroll's Appaloosa mare. Random had seen both before.

He had also seen the cold blue eyes that flicked with lazy indifference toward the passing riders and then widened in surprise. The last time Random had seen those eyes, they had been narrow and not cold—they had burned like beacons of hate over a handkerchief masking the boyish features.

The youth had been one of the four vigilantes who'd tried to murder Eulógio Gonzalez.

The gun toter stood as if his boot heels were glued to the wooden stoop in front of the *cantina*. With his

jet black hair, his pale eyes looked almost unnatural.
Never a sensitive man, Carroll continued into the
street without noticing his companion's discomfiture.

"You're just the man I was looking for, Random,"
he said. "Mr. Tanner's been rounding up men for
that there patrol you wanted to set up, and he ain't
even asked Cal Sharper, here. Says you'd turn him
down flat. Why's that? Cal is a good boy. Knows how
to treat the Mexes, too."

Random knew how Sharper treated Mexes, all
right, but he certainly wasn't going to tell Carroll
how he knew. The kid knew, all right; Random
could tell that he was itching with the desire to draw
his gun and avenge the humiliation the blond-haired
stranger had dealt him the day before. "Mr. Tanner
is right," Random said evenly. "I do not want any
children, even if they happen to be carrying dangerous weapons."

He nudged the gray with his spurs and rode
straight past the expostulating Carroll. He could feel
young Sharper's strange blue eyes drilling holes in his
spine.

Hooves clopped and Bacon drew up beside him.
"What the hell was that about?" Random asked before the rancher could speak.

"That was a bad thing to do," Bacon said. "Carroll's mighty thick with that Sharper kid. And that
boy is one mean son of a bitch."

"I can see that he thinks he is."

"Oh, he is, all right," Bacon insisted. "Got into hot
water just last year for shooting a man dead down in
Santa Fe. He got out of it by claiming self-defense.
Anyway, the man he killed was a Mexican. Him and
Mr. Carroll feel the same 'bout them greasers." He
shot Random a sidelong glance. "Lot of people do,
hereabouts."

Random spat into the dust and spurred his horse
into a trot. He was in no mood for warnings. He
knew far better than Bacon could that Sharper would

be looking for the slightest opportunity to gun him
down.

In the dust behind Bacon looked hard after the
young mercenary. He was a hard one to figure. He
looked no older than the kid he'd just called a
"child." But it didn't take much to tell that Random
was a hard case deep down. His coolness was even
more scary in its way than Cal Sharper's bluster.

Right then, Bacon knew how it would be. There
would be trouble between the blue-coated youth and
the local kid with the two-gun gait. Bad trouble. Killing trouble.

It could go either way. Random was tough for all
that he talked like a foreigner or an Eastern college
professor, but Sharper was just plain mean. And Tag
Carroll was a powerful man, even if Clay Barnes and
Tanner had him outvoted at the moment.

Henry Bacon was a prudent man. He held back on
the reins and let Random draw well ahead of him.
He didn't care to be seen with the outsider too much.

Tanner was standing on the schoolhouse steps
when Random rode up. "We're waitin' on you," he
said. Random dismounted and followed the tall
rancher into the school.

The small wooden desks had been moved out, leaving the schoolhouse tenanted by a chalkboard, a fat-
gutted black stove, and the teacher's oaken desk
which had probably been too much trouble to move.
Random walked in and sat on the edge of the desk.
He looked over the assembly.

Sixteen local men lounged against the walls or sat
on the pine planking of the floor. The youngest
looked about Random's age, the oldest, fifty or so.
They all looked Random over with a variety of expressions, ranging from curiosity to indifference. One
or two even allowed themselves to look hopeful.
There was no sign of hostility whatever, just a
natural, healthy reserve.

It was a point in Random's favor that he was not

at all self-conscious about giving orders to men twice his age. As one of the youngest foreigners ever commissioned in the Legion, he had grown accustomed to commanding men who had been fighting battles before he was born. In this situation he did not have the iron discipline of the Legion—to which he himself had never taken well—to back him up. He would have to earn the respect of these men on his own.

He smiled when Tanner, primed by Clay Barnes, introduced him as Captain Random. "You wonder what you can do that has not already been tried," he said without preamble. "I can assure you that the next party of *gorras blancas* who ride out will have a surprise waiting for them wherever they go."

The men exchanged skeptical glances and a buzz of muttered comments. Random sat patiently until they settled back to listen to his explanation.

From a coat pocket Random produced the map he had spent the afternoon annotating. Holding it up against the chalkboard for everyone to see, he explained tersely how any group of raiders would almost be sure to leave the other village by one of three routes he had marked on the map. "This may all seem farfetched, but right here"—he stabbed the map with his pencil—"I found sign of a number of horsemen, laid since the last rain, which I am told fell two days before the Cranston murder. Now, following this arroyo backwards, you meet, here, one of the three main routes I marked in."

"We found those prints the day after Luke was killed," said one of the men. "Couldn't follow 'em 'cause somebody'd run his cattle up the arroyo. Muddied the trail all up."

Random nodded. "I found a boy with his cows in there today. It's lucky that set of tracks wasn't blotted out as well. They confirmed that the raiders use those trails for their attacks."

He folded the map. "What we do, then, is quite simple. Every night we place two men watching each trail. When the night riders come out, one man shadows them while the other hurries back here and brings the rest of us."

"And then we jump the bastards and wipe 'em out!" somebody volunteered enthusiastically.

Random winced. He stuck map and pencil back into one of the voluminous pockets of his coat. "No," he said. "We chase them off, spilling no more blood than necessary. That will not be much, either. The *gorras* are out for raiding and stealing, not getting shot. I'll bet they haven't the stomach for a brisk fight."

The man who had spoken stood up. "I don't see no sense to that," he complained. "If we got 'em in our sights, why in hell don't we just finish them then and there?"

"What's your name?" Random asked.

"Marsh Balin."

"Well, Mr. Balin, that brings us to the second part of the problem. I can promise the *gorras* will, sooner or later, find a way past our patrols."

"Then what the hell good is all this botheration?" Balin demanded, asking the question for the entire group.

"It will give us time to stop the raids for good. And there is only one way to do that." He paused. "Do you, any of you, know why the raids started in the first place?"

"Nope," Balin said, shaking his head. "Us and the Mexes always got along good together."

"They are afraid of you," Random said. "They think some of you want to take their land away, so that the railroad will buy its right-of-way through here and make you—some of you—very rich."

"Nobody here, mister," Balin told him. "This here's our home. Besides, the only man here who owned any land the railroad wanted was Tanner, and he turned them down flat."

Random looked at the iron-haired rancher with

new respect. "It's my home, too," said Tanner. Random nodded.

"Whether or not the danger is real, the fear is. But the reason behind the raids is that there is a man who can play on that fear. He's convinced the natives that you want to rob them of their land—which I hear has happened quite often in the Territory. He has told them that the way to protect their homes is to assert their manhood by riding against their neighbors. By running you off before you can do the same to them."

Random rubbed an itch in his nose. He sat back down on the corner of the desk, wishing he had a drink of water. He still had trail dust in this throat. "This man is not just the leader of the *gorras blancas*: He's the only reason they exist. Without him the natives would nurse their grudges in private. He is the one who fires them to action. He is the head and heart of the night riders." Random paused for effect.

"So what happens if you remove him?"

His listeners looked at each other. "The *gorras* fold their hands," said a stocky man leaning against the wall. He had not spoken before, and seemed to hold himself apart from the others. "Unless."

"Unless?"

"Unless the natives stay scared of us. Or get mad. Then they'll have the gumption to pick up where their leader left off."

Surprised, Random nodded. "That's right. That is the reason I want to run this my way. Instead of the way, say, Mr. Carroll might choose to do things."

"I don't get it, Mr. Random," said the towheaded youth who looked about Random's age. "I'm Dave Sherman," he added hastily.

"Do you have a brother, Mr. Sherman?" The youngster nodded. "What would you do if the *gorras* killed him?"

Sherman flushed. "Why, I'd get the lousy bastards! I'd fix 'em good, you can count on that."

Random gave him a grim, lopsided smile. "And if

you were a native, and the Anglos killed your brother?"

"I . . ." The boy gulped and nodded his head.

"That's it. If we can take out the leader of the night riders, we can probably put a simple stop to the raids. But if the blood begins to flow . . ." He shook his head. "You will have war between yourselves and the natives. Not just the hotheads who pull pillowcases over their heads and go riding off to show what big men they are. All of them. And it will never end. It never does."

Silence filled the room. After a moment, Random spoke again. "We begin tonight. Go home and get what gear you'll need. We'll sleep here tonight. Come back after supper and I will assign you to your patrols. If anybody wants out, speak up now." He waited. No one spoke. "Very well."

The men filed out into the dusk. Random breathed a sigh of relief. He had not really expected any serious problem. There was a danger no one knew how to deal with. The men of San Rael would follow anyone who moved right now. And, as was the *gorras* and their chief, they'd follow his lead as long as he could produce results. Still, there had been the chance of someone objecting to his youth, or to the idea of an outsider coming in and handing out orders. That danger was past now. Now all he had to do was produce.

The square type who had been leaning on the wall seemed to be hanging back. He watched Random as the younger man approached him and stuck out his hand. "Thank you for your assistance," Random told him.

The man looked puzzled. He took Random's hand and shook it in a firm, dry grasp. "My name's Gorman. Russ Gorman. What do you mean, thank me? What did I do?" His tone was wary as his eyes.

"I might have had a hard time convincing those men if you hadn't spoken up." Random shrugged.

"You said the same things I was going to. Coming from a local man, they sounded much better than they would from a wet-behind-the-ears outsider—who talks funny."

Gorman smiled briefly. Then the smile went away. "You really mean what you said about avoiding bloodshed?"

"Yes, I do. It's the only hope you've got."

"What is it to you, then?" Gorman challenged abruptly.

They were alone in the room, except for Tanner and the tardily arrived Bacon, who stood talking in the doorway. "I'll be honest," Random said. "I only get paid if the raids stop. And the only way to stop them is to take away the *gorras*' leader while he's still the one thing that keeps them happening."

Gorman stood and considered this, chewing the inside of his lower lip. He had a broad, honest face under a head of close-cropped, ·curly, red-brown hair, peppered with gray.

"What branch of service were you in, Mr. Gorman?" Random asked suddenly. Gorman cocked his head, taken by surprise. "Some of the others no doubt carried a rifle musket in the War, but you were a professional. It's written all over you. Cavalry?" He nodded at the rifle propped at Gorman's side, an old .45–70 Springfield of the kind known as the trap door, issued to the U. S. Cavalry. It had the same weather-beaten look as its owner.

"Cavalry," Gorman affirmed. "Sergeant of scouts." He stared down at the scuffed toes of his boots. "I was with Major Reno's outfit at Little Big Horn. In the woods."

Random was impressed. The battle known as Custer's Last Stand had made an enormous impression both in Europe and in the European colonies. Random had read all about it, including the hardships and heroism of the men who were pinned in a clump of trees by the Greasy Grass while Long Hair himself and two hundred some of his men paid the price of folly on a nearby hilltop. "You've got experience, then," he said, "and you know the country around here pretty well, don't you?" Gorman nodded.

"I need a second in command," Random said. "Will you take the job?"

A minute went by. "I'll do it," said Gorman at last, and went out the door carrying his rifle by the barrel.

Tanner and Bacon stepped aside to let him by. "He's a good man," Tanner said. "You made a good choice."

Bacon shook his head. "He's a funny one. Didn't expect to see him here." He sounded disapproving.

"Why not, Mr. Bacon?" Random asked.

"Think he's crazy," Bacon said frankly. "When he was mustered out of the Cavalry, he went around saying white folks shouldn't ought to take land what belonged to the Indians away from 'em." He shook his sad head at Gorman's wild notions. "Crazy, like I said. Anyways, after what he said about the night riders I thought sure he wouldn't be keen on helping you none."

"And just what did he say, Mr. Bacon?"

"Said he figgered it was about time the Mexes stood up for what was theirs."

CHAPTER FIVE

Random slept, but his sleep was not restful. In spite of the night's coolness there was sweat on his forehead. He tossed and turned beneath the rough blanket.

There was plenty on his mind to disturb his sleep. Sharper and three unknowns gunning for him. Tag Carroll thirsting for native blood, hunting the slightest excuse to trip him up and bring on the confrontation Random so feared. And Gorman: a second in command whom many San Raelites thought of as a renegade, a Mex-lover—who had publicly sympathized with the night riders.

Could Gorman be trusted? Random didn't feel it would be politic to reverse his appointment of the Cavalry veteran as his assistant. He had long ago learned that the premier military virtue was the ability to make decisions and stick by them. Also, he'd seen nothing to change his conviction that Gorman was the best man for the job.

All he could do now was sleep. Badly.

Devils chased each other through his dreams. He moaned, thrashed, kicked out. Then he awakened suddenly, sat up to find Gorman watching him.

"Nightmare?" Gorman asked.

"Yes."

Gorman rolled a cigarette and lit a match. A coal glowed into life at the tip of the cigarette. "Smoke?"

Random shook his head. He felt drained, ill.

The two men tensed at the same instant. From outside came a hint of noise, the urgent drumming of horses' hooves on hardpan. Random climbed to his feet. Gorman was gone, materializing out of the darkness in a moment with his Springfield in hand as Random reached the door of the schoolhouse. He followed the young man out.

Dave Sherman was just turning off the road with his sorrel blowing hard. He was one of the six men Random had assigned to watch the trails this first night. He reined in as he saw the pair on the schoolhouse steps. "They're coming!"

Horse and horsemen's breath blew white in the darkness. The animals were running fast and quiet. Random, Gorman, and five others rode in purposeful silence, with young Sherman in the head to guide the way.

Sherman and his partner, Webb Gordon, had been watching the easternmost trail—a wide arroyo—when a party of eight horsemen had passed. The bank was crumbling, so the raiders took their horses along the flat bottom. Sherman and Webb had watched them from cover, reins wrapped around their own horses' noses to prevent a betraying whicker of greeting to the *gorras'* mounts.

The youthful Anglos had followed, carefully staying well back and out of sight, for half a mile. Webb was certain the night riders were heading for the Morris homestead to the northeast of town. Two ranches on either side of the Morris location had been hit in the last two months, the Morrises, never. Sherman had gone at a gallop for help.

With their need for stealth, the White Hoods would be traveling slowly now, as they approached their target. Random's men had no such concern. They ran their horses full out. Sherman steered them north and east, following a trail until they came to an arroyo that he said cut across a corner of Sam Morris' property.

Here the Anglos employed the *gorra* trick of following a wash. Hidden in the deep narrow cut, their hoofbeats muffled by sand, they could take the raiders totally by surprise—if they could reach them before they struck.

The troop rounded a bend. Revolvers cocked and horses reared as a rider loomed up before them. "Don't shoot!" the newcomer hissed. "Webb. Came ahead. It's the Morris place, all right."

Random signaled a halt. His big shotgun was in his hand, and the collar of his coat was pulled up against the cold. "How far to the house?"

"Hundred yards or so. Come up from this arroyo, go through a stand of trees, and there you are. The Mexes're on the other side, sneakin' up slowlike. Think they aim to clear out the corral. Sam's got him some fine horseflesh in there."

"That's how we'll go, then. Spread out and go in fast. Burn up all the cartridges you want—they're paid for—but don't shoot *at* anyone unless you have to." The men nodded agreement. Random was in command and no one doubted it. He looked at their shadowed faces, star-glinting rifles. "*Allons!* We go!"

Webb led them over the top at a place where the cutbank had caved in. The horses slipped but made it quietly, without mishap. Featureless dark trees reached skyward ahead of them. The riders were fanning out as they rode in among the pines.

They knew the country and were all experienced horsemen. Random trusted them to make as little noise as possible. The trees gave way to a clearing, in the center of which lay a silent house, windows black and empty like a skull's eyes.

Something stirred in the clearing. A bent-over human figure, head pale and bobbing against the blackness. With a thrill Random knew he was seeing the *gorra blanca* for which the marauders were named. The raider crept toward the house. More white blobs were moving on the other side of the clearing by the adobe-walled corral. Random could not see what they were doing. Later he would learn they were using the Apache trick of wetting the mud brick and sawing it with a long hair from a horse's tail.

A horse snorted and whickered in the enclosure. Inside the dwelling someone chose that instant to awaken. A match flared behind a window, gave way to the glow of a kerosene lamp. Someone was heading for the front door.

The White Hood crossing the yard halted, raised a blunt carbine.

"Yaiii-yi-yi-yi!" Random howled, spurring the gray as he fired one barrel of the shotgun straight into the air. A flash like lightning lit the clearing as the shot boomed. The mare lunged headlong and shattered branches rained at her heels.

The *gorra* was up and running like a madman. His comrades milled and yelled in confusion. The light went out in the house as the lantern bearer hit the floorboards, frightened by the stage-gun's roar and Random's battle cry.

On either side, Random's riders were screaming. Gunfire crackled and Random prayed they were aiming high. Then flame blossomed across the clearing. A bullet cracked by Random, and his mare went crazy with a squeal of pain.

His hat flew off as he fought to control the plunging animal. He felt warm blood on his face. The horse had been hit, he didn't know where. But she was out of control, and he was suddenly very vulnerable, out in the open.

From the corner of his eye he saw a mounted White Hood detach himself from the shadows. Starlight gleamed from a rifle as the native aimed. Desperately Random loosed the other barrel of his shotgun. The *gorra* was out of range of the rapidly spreading pellets, but Random hoped the shot would put off the rifleman's aim.

The *gorra* hesitated. *Where the hell are the others?* Random thought wildly. He could hear but not see his men. His night vision was gone anyway from the muzzle flash of the shotgun. With his mare bucking and sunfishing he was helpless—and doomed, if the night rider could draw a bead on him.

The mare's forelegs came off the ground. Random hung on, feeling the *gorra*'s gun following him. When the beast pawed air at the top of her rear the gunman would blow him out of the saddle.

The mare poised on her hind legs. Random bit his lip. Then a rifle went off at his side with a doomsday roar and a huge blaze of fire. The raider sagged in his saddle, dropping his weapon. Two San Rael men hurtled shouting past Random as Gorman, smoking Springfield in one hand, caught the mare's bridle and dragged her head down.

"Thanks!" Random yelled. Gorman's mount was prancing nervously at the smell of horse blood, making guttural sounds of fear. "I'm okay—get those men back! We've driven them off!"

Gorman charged away. Random hauled back on the reins. Abruptly, the mare sat down. Random's boots came clear of the stirrups and their soles thudded on the ground. The horse gathered herself and eeled right out from between her rider's legs, leaving him to stand sheepishly alone.

Feeling like a total idiot, Random watched the injured mare disappear into the forest in three bounds. Then he heard the house door open. Metal clicked.

Slowly he turned. A woman stood in the doorway, clad in a nightgown, her mouth set in a grim line. She was pointing a big Sharps rifle at him.

Random put up his hands. As badly as he had botched his part in the night's action, it was only natural for him to be shot by the people he was trying to help. The woman peered at him from under ferocious, unplucked eyebrows.

"My God, Sarah!" a man's voice exclaimed. "Put

that down! That there's a white man, sure as the day
you were born!"

The woman lowered the buffalo gun. Random
bowed to her with a sardonic flourish.

"Good evening, madame," he said. "Sorry to have
disturbed you."

CHAPTER SIX

The *nativo* village of San Rael was, on the outside, not very different from its Anglo counterpart. The clustered buildings were a shade shabbier, there were fewer commercial structures, and more small adobe dwellings. On a hill overlooking the town was a church with thick clay walls, reminiscent of a time when the church also served as a fortress in case of attack: the old *Cristo Redentor* mission, Random had been told, that had been the focal point for the original settlement of San Rael. As Random rode into the village, a bell was tolling in the tower. A meadowlark sang, perched on a white wooden cross in the little cemetery next to the mission.

His mare had a strange look to her this morning, owing to the bulky bandage wrapped around her right ear. The *gorra blanca* rifleman's first shot had gone cleanly through it. It was not a serious wound, but it had been painful enough to make the beast run amok.

This particular morning, Random's was the only white face to be seen on the *caliche* street. The brown faces he encountered turned to him with blankness or hostility. He met both with polite nods, and when he passed, people would stand looking after him.

It had been some time since a lone Anglo had ridden into the village.

The Mexican settlement was more structured than the Anglo one. It centered on the *plaza*, an empty

square of sun-baked red earth. On market or feast
days, the *plaza* teemed with townsfolk and people
down from the mountains; now it was almost abandoned. A few loungers turned their heads to stare at
the intruder as Random reined his horse up by a gar-
ishly pink building that fronted on the square.

The *cantina* was smaller than Turk's, in the other
town. From inside came a buzz of conversation and
the pungent smells of native cooking. Random dismounted and tethered the gray to a hitching bar.
From behind his saddle he removed a slender linen-
wrapped bundle which he tucked under his arm.
Then he strode into the *cantina*.

The conversation seemed to twitch once and die
gradually as heads turned to take in the newcomer. It
was dim in here, and despite the fact that outside was
warming toward a hot spring noon, the air was suddenly chill.

At a table in the middle of the room were five
young *nativos*. Their faces were wooden but their
eyes glittered with hate as Random strode up and de-
posited his bundle on the table.

The men tensed. Among them was Roberto Morales, sitting with his back to the door. His handsome
face darkened and his lip curled as the youthful
gringo untied the rawhide thongs that secured the
bundle.

Random pulled away the cloth to reveal a gleaming new Winchester with a silver-chased receiver and
a blond wood stock. It was a beautiful, expensive
piece of workmanship. "Good morning," he said,
standing back. "Does anyone know to whom this be-
longs?"

For a moment he could practically hear his listeners deciding whether they spoke English. Finally one
of them, with a glance at Roberto, spoke up. *"Sí,"* he
said slowly. "It is the property of Esteban Montoya."

The air temperature had dropped a few more
degrees. "Will you please see that he gets it, señor?"

Random asked politely. "He must miss it very badly."

Everyone in the *cantina* was concentrating on the little tableau. "Esteban Montoya is dead, señor," the native said stiffly. "He died this morning." The youths crossed themselves.

Random's face was solemn. "I am sorry to hear that. How did it happen?"

A mutter of low Spanish syllables passed along the five. Roberto gave Random a heated look, but the spokesman silenced him with a gesture. "A hunting accident. Only last night. *Que lástima,*" he said.

"A pity," Random agreed, hands thrust into the pockets of his long *capote*. "Hunting at night is often hazardous, is it not? Please return the rifle to his family with my regrets. *Adiós.*" He touched his hat and walked out the door without a backward glance.

Once in the saddle he looked back to see Roberto in the doorway. The youth seemed to want to say something, but he seemed to have difficulty finding the words.

"A tragedy," Random told him. "It may be that you can prevent a repetition of it, my friend."

Roberto stood glaring as he rode away. As Random passed the adobe church he allowed himself a small smile of triumph. Then he spurred the mare into a long, easy lope and was gone.

Cheerfully, the meadowlark warbled from his perch.

The morning's next errand was no easier, but it was far safer. The first had brought him face to face with at least five of the White Hoods, and he had come away intact.

It was the same sort of calculated madness that had won him his reputation in Algeria. His trademark was to walk right up to his enemy, greet him, and then walk away. If he got away, and he always had, he knew that enemy could never again face him with complete calm. Random knew how to touch his foe like a Plains Indian counting coup, besting him at something he could perceive but not understand.

If he failed, ever, there was the knife or the bullet. Random's hands were shaking, a little, but he felt good. He'd pulled it off, just as he had in the old days. And he was sure the *gorras* were already talking excitedly about the fearless Anglo, brazenly bringing back the rifle dropped by the raider Russ Gorman had shot the night before.

Now, however, he had the unpleasant task of facing Eulógio Gonzalez and telling him the truth about what he was doing in San Rael. And Random had to convince the older man to help him do it.

The first shot had been fired in the battle to the death between Random and Noe Villareal. Before it was finished, Random would need all the allies he could get, *nativo* as well as white.

Gonzalez was repairing a broken rail in his corral with Joselito's mute assistance. The native wiped sweat from his forehead and waved a greeting when Random rode into view. "*Buenos dias*," Gonzalez called. "What brings you here this morning, *amigo?*"

"I must speak with you," Random said. "I just returned Esteban Montoya's fine rifle to his friends."

"Was it lost?" Gonzalez asked. "It is a lovely weapon. His father gave it to him for his confirmation. Señor Montoya is wealthy, for a *nativo*. It is sad about the accident."

"It was no accident," Random said grimly, swinging down from the saddle. "He was shot last night in a raid on the Morris ranch. The boy had a white hood over his head, and he was shooting that pretty carbine at me. That is why I must talk to you."

Gonzalez' dark face showed pain. "So you have become involved in our troubles after all," he said.

"More than you think, señor."

The native told Joselito, who stood by stone-faced as ever, to carry on with the repairs. He walked into the house. Random followed.

"Señor Random!" a female voice exclaimed as he stepped into the *sala*. The room was dark and smelled of *piñon* smoke. "You have come back to visit us."

"Leave us, Elena," Gonzalez said. "Señor Random and I must talk together as man to man."

The girl started to rebel, but the look on her father's face made her turn and go out without speaking. Gonzalez sat and motioned his guest to do the same.

Random laid hat and coat on the *banco* and found a chair. He refused refreshment. "When I've said my piece you may wish you had never broken bread with me," he said.

"You saved my life, my friend," Gonzalez said. "Say what you have come to say."

Random took a deep breath. "The other night you did not ask my purpose in coming to San Rael. I allowed you to assume I was merely a traveler passing through. I am not. I am a professional soldier. I came because the Anglos hired me to stop the raid by the *gorras blancas*."

"Are you telling me you are my enemy, señor?" Gonzalez asked after a pause. "You did save my life."

"I am not your enemy," Random said, leaning forward. "I would not take money to drive the *nativos* from their homes. I am here to stop the raids, and I shall."

"Why did you not tell me that first night?"

"How could I? I was not even certain I would keep the job. My employers might have wanted other methods than mine."

"*Qué*—what methods are these?"

"I thought they might insist on riding to your village to teach your people a 'lesson' with torch and rope. How well would that work, señor?"

"The fools." Gonzalez shook his head. "My people would fight them forever."

"Exactly. You see, it is not only my . . . sympathy for the *nativos* that makes me reject such methods. That sort of idiocy would make my task impossible."

"Then how will you stop the *gorras*?"

"I need help. That is why I came. I need you to help me."

The older man's expression did not change. He sat, quietly regarding his guest. "I cannot betray my people," he said at length, "even to repay a debt such as I owe you."

"I would not presume to ask that. On this you have my word of honor."

"We *latinos* take honor very seriously."

"So do I, señor."

Gonzalez sighed. "We have as much to gain as the Anglos, if the *gorras* are made to quit," he said. "And you risked your life to save mine. The life of a Mexican." He shrugged. "I trust you. What do you wish of me?"

Random told him.

The old man leaned on his shovel. His face was seamed and weathered by the changes three quarters of a century had brought. Placidly, he smoked a cigarette and watched the muddy water trickle into his field.

A shout drew his attention. He looked up to see a stout figure approaching him on the back of a fine bay gelding. He recognized the ditch *mayordomo,* the man entrusted by the natives with making sure each farmer took only the water apportioned to him, and with keeping the *acequias* clear of weeds and free flowing.

"*Hola,* Eulógio," he called. "*Buenas tardes.*"

"*Buenas,* Amadeo." Gonzalez reined his horse to a stop on the ditchbank. "How are your beans growing?"

"The first sprouts appeared yesterday morning.

They are fine and healthy. This will be a good year, the Blessed Virgin willing." He crossed himself.

"That is so." Gonzalez also made the sign of the Cross. "But evil times have come to San Rael. There is much violence in the air. If the winds blow up, they will shrivel your fine bean plants like the *santana* from the desert, *amigo*."

"True," Amadeo said. He cackled. "What about these youngsters, these *gorras blancas*? They're lighting a fire under these *cabrones gringos, qué no*?"

Gonzalez nodded. "True enough, *viejo*. But is it then such a good thing, to light a fire under our neighbors? We have lived in peace with them for years, Amadeo."

The oldster frowned. He spat out a fragment of tobacco, then sucked noisily on the butt and tossed it away into the furrowed field. "Eh, *cuate*, we have lived with them a long time. But these *gorras!* Reminds me of the war with the Americans, when I fought with Manuel Armijo—"

"Manuel Armijo did not fight the Americans. He took from them ten thousand dollars in gold and withdrew his troops from ambush in Apache Canyon without firing a shot." Gonzalez paused to allow the oldster to roll another cigarette. He marveled at the deftness of the gnarled, ancient fingers. "Is fighting what we want? Did you have any reason to hate Luke Cranston?"

A match hissed as Amadeo lit his cigarette. "No. Luke was a good man. When my granddaughter Isabel was in bad labor, he rode all the way to Los Duranes in a blizzard to bring a doctor, because Doctor Stern was in Santa Fe. No one had any reason to hate him, except he was a *gringo*."

"But these *gorras* you admire, they killed him."

"That is so."

"And what if the *gorras* keep killing Anglos? Will not the horse soldiers come? Will they not ride through your fine fields and trample your bean sprouts? Might not a stray bullet hit one of your great-grandchildren? How about the lovely girl your Isabel bore two months ago—if war comes to San Rael, will she be safe?"

Amadeo scratched behind one ear. "I do not know, Eulógio," he admitted. "These White Hoods are brash young men whose *cojones* perhaps grow too large for their trousers. It may be as you say. They may bring grief to our village."

"Perhaps you older men should get together," Gonzalez suggested. "You could use the wisdom of your years on this problem."

"You could be right, Eulógio. I believe you are."

"Come to my home tomorrow night, then. The *viejos* will meet there to discuss the night riders."

Amadeo considered it. "I will come," he said. "We old men have stood by in silence long enough. It is time we stopped this foolishness, *qué no?*"

"You are a wise man, Amadeo. *Adiós.*"

"*Vaya con Dios.* Go with God." The stout man rode away. Amadeo watched him go, thinking, *what a good and sensible young man this Eulógio Gonzalez is!* Too many youngsters scoffed at the older men. He puffed contentedly on his cigarette and began to spade dirt back into the channel to check the flow of water into his field.

All afternoon Eulógio Gonzalez rode the hills around San Rael, seeking out *los viejos,* the grandfathers and great-grandfathers of the village.

"Will you come to my house tomorrow, Juan?" he asked here.

"The young men are laughing at you, Miguel," he said there. "They call you *vieja,* old woman, for warning that this night riding will bring no good to San Rael. Come to my *casa....*"

Again, he said: "The *gorras* made you shelter them in your barn, Seferino? They are out of control. They are our enemies as much as any Anglo, *qué no?* Tomorrow night, we meet...."

And finally, as the sun slid down toward the peaks and shadows crept over the land, Gonzalez sought out a much younger man.

"You spoke to me after Luke Cranston was murdered, José Pacheco," he said. "You still believe the *gorras* are wrong? Yet you ride with them."

Pacheco turned away from the older man. "I am afraid, Eulógio. *El Jefe* would kill me if I tried to quit. I do not know what to do. The burning, the running off of cows and horses—once I thought these things could help us. But murder, Eulógio! Luke Cranston was a friend of the *nativos*. The *gorras blancas* are as evil and ruthless as *El Jefe* tells us the *gringos* are."

"Would you help stop the raids, then?"

Pacheco eyed him warily. "You ask me to betray them? Many are still my friends. It is *El Jefe* who is evil."

"If *El Jefe* were taken away, would they still ride?"

"No," Pacheco confessed. "He is as persuasive as Satan himself, that one. Were it not for him, the White Hoods would stay at home at night by the warmth of their hearths."

"Then go to the Anglo town. There is a man there, a man named Random. Help him capture the chief."

"A *gringo*! Me help a *gringo*?"

"This *gringo* is a good man," Gonzalez said. "He was hired to stop the raids—"

"How can I help a *gringo* gunfighter?"

"But he saved me from four masked Anglos who wanted to hang me. He is our friend, I am sure of this. But he is determined to stop the night riders. He believes that if their leader is removed, the raids will stop with little bloodshed, by us or the Anglos. You fear and hate *El Jefe*. Will you not help destroy him?"

Pacheco looked down at his booted feet scuffing the earth of San Rael. Somewhere, deep inside, he felt a premonition. "I must think about it, Eulógio," he said. "I must think about it for a long time."

CHAPTER SEVEN

A little after noontime, Russ Gorman sauntered into Turk's *cantina* for a few shots of Bushmill's Irish Whiskey, from a bottle Turk kept especially for him and old McMurphey, proprietor of the general store across the thoroughfare. The bottle was well shy of a quarter full, so he paid for the contents and took it to a table.

He was scarcely settled down to his drinking when the double doors flew open and Cal Sharper and several of his friends came in. They were all high-stepping young bravos, but each deferred to Sharper, who strutted up to the bar like a fighting cock. He ordered his shot, leaned on one elbow on the bar, and tossed it off. His pale eyes took in the dimly lit room. They fixed on Gorman, sitting by himself and ignoring the crowd of rowdy youngsters.

"Well, now, boys, I hear this new fella chased off a bunch of Mexes last night," Sharper said loudly. "Maybe he's figgered it out that the only way to deal with them lousy chilibellies is to give 'em a good dose of lead whenever they step out of line."

He glanced at the former scout, who still ignored him. In the gloom he couldn't see how Gorman's fingers were clenched tightly around the Bushmill's bottle. "Also hear tell our Mr. Random is ridin' around the Mextown at this very minute, off to pay a social call to some of his greaser friends." Sharper looked around at his cronies.

"That is the very way I heard it. 'Friends.' Don't

that beat damn all? This boy we hired to protect us from the Mexes, pallin' around with 'em like they was his long-lost brothers." The others muttered darkly, nodding.

At his table, Gorman stiffened. Random had let his employers and his men know he was trying to enlist help from the *nativos* themselves. But it wouldn't do to have it noised around. How had Sharper found out about it?

"And another thing," Sharper drawled, turning and leaning back with both elbows on the bar, "this Random has got him a sidekick name of Gorman. This here Mr. Gorman has been known to say he figgers the Mexes oughta stand up for their rights. He likes the dirty greasers. But this Mr. Gorman now, he's supposed to be helping Mr. Random fight the night riders. Ain't that the funniest thing?" He looked directly at the ex-Cavalryman. "Ain't that strange, *Mister* Gorman?"

Gorman looked the boy right in the eye. It gave him a chill down the spine. There was something not right about Cal Sharper. Something that made him as dangerous as he made himself out to be.

"I said the natives should stand up for their rights," Gorman said evenly, taking a sip of his drink. "The whites throughout the Territory treat 'em like dirt. Why shouldn't they do something about it?"

"Why don't you pull a pillowcase over your head and go ridin' with 'em?"

"All the *gorras* are good for is giving young horses' asses like yourselves a chance to act tough. Wasn't for men like Tanner and Clay Barnes, you would have started a full-scale war between the two bunches of you." He spat into the sawdust on the floor. "Fact is, you buckos are just exactly like the *gorras*. No better and no worse."

He stood up, picked up the whiskey bottle by the neck, and drained off half of what was left. Then he strode to the bar. His path led between Sharper and one of his partners. The other kid moved to block him, and Gorman shouldered him aside.

"Here, Turk," Gorman said, slamming the bottle down. "Have yourself a drink on me. This stuff don't taste so good all of a sudden. Something in the air, I reckon."

He turned away. The kid he'd jostled stood with his hand hovering over the butt of his gun. His chin was stuck out belligerently. "Go ahead, son," Gorman said cheerfully. "Go right ahead and shoot. It's safe, I ain't armed."

The youngster stared at him. Scowling, Sharper shook his head. Gorman walked off with the youth glaring at his broad back.

As Gorman left the *cantina* another lone drinker stirred at his table in the dark corner. He upset his whiskey bottle, grabbed at it and missed, and cursed savagely when it rolled off onto the floor. It didn't break, and only a few drops dribbled out into the sawdust. The man stood, steadied himself on the table edge, and lurched toward the door.

"Hey, old Shorty!" Sharper called, noticing the man for the first time. "You really done tied one on, ain't you?"

Shorty drew himself up with drunken dignity. "What d'you 'spect?" he demanded. "A man kin only stomach so much of this kow—kow-towing to them Mexes. Enough to drive a body to—hic!—drink."

"Sure 'nough is, Shorty. It purely is."

Straightening his hat, Shorty staggered out through the door into the street. He stopped and stood blinking into the bright sunlight.

Fifty yards up the street, Gorman was walking in the direction of the schoolhouse. Shaking his head in what looked like alcoholic befuddlement, the man called Shorty studied his surroundings from beneath his hat brim. There was no one else in sight.

The other drinkers in Turk's *cantina*, and the shaven-headed, burly Turk himself, had seen him getting well and truly soaked in his dark corner. They could testify to it in a court of law if necessary.

Of course, since the corner had been so dark, none of them had any way of knowing most of the vast amounts of whiskey Shorty had purchased that day had soaked into the sawdust covering the *cantina* floor. While he wanted to look drunk, for what he was about to do he needed to be cold sober.

He smiled a little to himself, out there in the sunlight. He was a local boy, after all. And if he gunned down a complete stranger—well, hell, everybody had seen Shorty; he was drunk as a louse that day. And if Mr. high and mighty Random, who thought he could come into San Rael and tell us how to deal with these yellow-bellied greasers—if he'd let himself be taken out by a drunken man, what the hell good was he, anyway? A jury would understand. Twelve local boys wouldn't penalize one of their own too heavily for shooting some Mex-loving outsider.

And even if they would, arrangements had been made. Random wasn't the only one with influential friends.

The object of this exercise was standing in McMurphey's with his blue-coated back to the door and a pile of goods stacked beside him as he stood at the counter checking off a list of supplies. He heard the door open and a booted foot fall on the floorboards. He glanced casually over his shoulder.

With the light to his back, the newcomer's features were indistinct. But his short, stumpy form was familiar, as was the revolver he wore at his hip.

It was an unusual make of weapon, a double-action Colt, .41 caliber, the kind advertised as the Thunderer.

Random had found another of the four masked men. Or, rather, this one had found him.

Shorty took a step inside, reeling slightly. Random could smell the whiskey fumes from where he stood. "Morning to you, Shorty," the round little Irishman

McMurphey said cheerfully. "And it's a fine day we have, thank the Lord."

" 'Sallright," Shorty slurred, "till I whiffed the stink of Mex-lover. Spoiled the day right off." He wiped his mouth with the back of his hand, glaring at Random with mean pig eyes.

"Now, Shorty, don't be makin' trouble. Ye've had a bit too much to drink. Why don't you be goin' and sleepin' it off, there's a good lad?"

Shorty took his hand from his mouth and dropped it deliberately to his side. Random took a step to the side, away from the pink-cheeked shopkeeper. "Don't give me that crap, McMurphey. This here Random's been sellin' his own white kind down the river. Time somebody did something about it."

The eyes staring at Random were not the eyes of a drunken man. In the hard-drinking Legion, Random had seen enough truly inebriated men to recognize when one was faking.

Shorty took two steps forward, coming to stand three feet away from Random. Despite the alcoholic reek, Random knew he was sober. Everything suddenly became clear.

Shorty meant to murder him. Had planned it.

"Mr. McMurphey's right, Shorty," Random said easily. His voice betrayed none of the tension he felt. "Why not just follow his advice, go home and—"

The cowhand moved.

By now two hundred yards away on the main street of San Rael, Russ Gorman was brought up short by the sound of three shots, coming so fast they seemed to blend into one. In front of the general store he saw Random's gray roan whinny and kick at the sound of gunfire. He turned back and raced down the street as men poured out of Turk's.

Sharper and company got to the store long before Gorman and started to crowd inside. They fell back just as rapidly. Gorman came up, shouldered his way through, and stepped into the store.

It was dark. The room was filled with an acrid haze of gunsmoke. Just inside the door Cal Sharper stood and stared, openmouthed. By the counter, Random stood with his feet spread wide, aiming his cocked Peacemaker at the black-haired young tough.

Slumped against the wall was an inert, oddly shapeless form. Gorman had seen sufficient corpses to recognize this as one. Its plaid shirt smoldered from the blast of a firearm a handsbreadth away.

In the middle of the floor a gun was spinning slowly on one side. It was a shiny Colt Thunderer.

There was a commotion at Gorman's back. Hoopwright came in, coughing at the smoke. "What's going on here?" he demanded.

"Sheriff, arrest this man!" Sharper exclaimed, a shrill edge to his voice. "He's murdered Shorty Kring!"

"Cause of death, three bullets fired from a large-caliber handgun at a range of from eight to eighteen inches. Two shots passed through the heart; the third narrowly missed the left auricle but ruptured a pulmonary artery. Any of the shots could have been fatal in and of itself; death was instantaneous." Dr. Stern removed his spectacles and polished them with his handkerchief while a pimply faced youth took down his dictation. "Your protestations to the contrary notwithstanding, Mr. Random, it seems you are something of a gunfighter. Don't take that down, Freddie, for God's sake."

The pimply kid looked up in dismay. Random couldn't help noticing a certain familial resemblance to the sheriff, who sat behind his desk looking unhappy. "What I meant," Random said, "was that I am no gunslinger like Clay Allison or John Wesley Harding. But I have used a pistol before."

"Obviously," Dr. Stern agreed. He permitted himself a grim smile. "Do you have the proper forms, Zebedee?"

Hoopwright grubbed in his desk, then shook his head and disappeared into the recesses of the warehouse. The smell of hides was rank through the open door. Random sat at ease and looked at the doctor. "May I ask you a question, Dr. Stern?"

"Certainly."

"I don't wish to ask you to violate any confidences. But I'm curious. What happened to Mr. Barnes? Sometimes he seems quite well, and other times he's in pain."

"Didn't Junel—Miss Barnes—tell you?" The doctor looked surprised.

"A little. Something about a back injury."

Stern nodded. "There's little more to say, actually. It must have been five, six months ago he had a riding accident." He looked thoughtful. "Medical science is advancing rapidly, but we still don't know much about back injuries. They can have a great deal of effect or none at all. The symptoms can come and go, change, intensify, disappear forever."

He replaced his glasses on the bridge of his nose. "It's a good thing Clay's heart is sound," he said. "The news about Shorty will hit him hard. Shorty is—was—one of Clay Barnes's wranglers."

Random looked thoughtfully at him. Hoopwright returned with a sheaf of papers. "Here's the form," he said. "Death by misadventure. That it?"

"That is correct." Stern glanced at Random. "It's up to you as sheriff to determine whether it was self-defense or not. Shorty never fired his gun, I'm told."

"McMurphey saw it plain as day. Old Shorty drew first. The Mick says he's never seed a man throw down faster'n this Random. Afore you could blink, he had that Colt shoulder high and blasting." Hoopwright gazed at Random with admiration. "Mister, I always figgered that reverse-draw stuff was fancy-pants nonsense for Eastern dudes. Guess you showed me different."

Random was far less calm that he appeared. He

was not worried about what would happen to him. But he was badly shaken, almost sick. His mouth was dry and his tongue felt like a wadded-up wool blanket. He had not killed a man since he'd left the Legion. He'd almost forgotten what it was like. It wasn't pleasant.

Hoopwright sat regarding him. "Now that's taken care of," he said slowly, "I reckon we got some other business to tend to. Stand up, son, and raise your right hand."

Surprised, Random complied with the sheriff's request. He'd no sooner finished repeating the words Hoopwright asked him to than the office's front door opened with a bang.

Junella Barnes stood there. She was dressed to kill in a high-necked pink dress and masses of crinoline, with her golden hair piled atop her head and covered by a wide, impractical hat. "What is going on in here?" she demanded. "Where are you keeping Mr. Ran—oh, hello." Her eyes had taken a moment to accustom themselves to the gloom of the sheriff's office.

"What are you holding him for?" she asked Hoopwright.

"Well, uh, we're not—"

"I demand that you release him immediately. It is a blot on the Barnes family honor that one of our trusted employees tried so treacherously to murder this gentleman. It is an affront to my guardian, who is a respected member of this community, for you to hold Mr. Random prisoner for rightfully defending himself."

It was a fine little speech and she had obviously gone to some trouble to prepare it. Withering under the girl's angry gaze, Hoopwright said, "Well, ma'am, we wasn't rightly holding him at all. We got Mr. McMurphey's sworn affydavit that Shorty drew first."

"Then why are you detaining Mr. Random?"

"Sheriff Hoopwright has just sworn Mr. Random in as deputy," the doctor said smoothly. "He hopes to avoid similar misunderstandings in the future. A wise move, in my estimation."

Junella stopped protesting and looked, first at the doctor, then at Hoopwright, and finally at Random, who picked up his hat and coat. "I appreciate your concern, Miss Barnes," he said. He offered his arm.

"Good afternoon, gentlemen." He nodded politely to Hoopwright and Dr. Stern. Then, with Junella Barnes's gloved and dainty hand on his arm, he strolled into the afternoon sun.

CHAPTER EIGHT

"You got to watch that Sharper kid," Gorman said later that afternoon. Random smiled.

"I already have, Russ. Picked him as a bad one from the start. I won't let him get behind me, never fear."

The stocky scout shook his head. "Not what I meant. I mean, he's liable to go stirring up trouble with the *nativos*. He could ruin all you're aimin' for—he's the kind of skunk who thinks a man ain't got the same colored skin as him's as fair game as mule deer."

"I know." Random paced slowly across the floor of the schoolhouse, watching dust motes float in the yellow afternoon light pouring in the windows. "But it may not be my concern very much longer."

He jerked his head in the direction of the stately Barnes house across the road. Inside the six men who had initially decided to summon him to San Rael were holding a conclave. The subject was whether his services would be required any longer or not. The killing of Shorty Kring was not the sort of thing that could go unnoticed. Random knew he was actually doing something about the raids for the first time, but whether his employers would decide that weighed more heavily than his killing a white he couldn't say. He knew how Carroll would vote; the others he didn't care to guess at.

"I have a feeling that'd bother you a bunch," Gorman said. He sat in a chair tipped back against the wall.

"You're right. I have a thousand dollars riding on what goes on in that house. I'd be very bothered if I lost it."

Gorman shook his head. "That wouldn't be all."

"Wouldn't it?"

"No." The front legs of the chair thumped onto the floorboards. "You got more of a stake than just money in this thing. You want to see the right thing done."

"You really think so?"

"If I didn't," Gorman said deliberately, "I never would've saved your bacon last night at the Morris place."

Random laughed.

They heard a knock on the door. Dave Sherman stuck his head in. "They'd like to talk to you over 'cross the way, Mr. Random," he said.

Random looked at Gorman. The ex-scout shrugged. Random picked up his hat and followed Sherman across the road.

The minute he walked in he knew which way it had gone. Tag Carroll sat to one side looking like a sulky schoolboy; Tanner and Stern looked pleased, and Clay Barnes was like a cat in cream. The young man couldn't help noticing the cane propped beside Barnes's chair, however.

There was a short discussion. Random had to make one concession he disliked. From now on he must give his employers daily progress reports. Having to account so closely for his actions annoyed him, but if it made the men who had hired him feel they were in control, so they left him with a reasonably free hand, so much the better.

He stood by as the men left. Barnes climbed painfully to his feet, shrugging off the younger man's assistance. "This damned back of mine is acting up again," he said. He steadied himself with the cane.

"You have no idea how much this whole shameful business mortifies me, Mr. Random."

"Think nothing of it."

"I do. I shall. But I am glad this meeting went as it did. I want you to know I have every confidence in you."

Random thanked him. Then Lacey appeared and helped Barnes into the foyer and up the stairs. He looked years older than the day before, Random thought.

Junella entered as Random was making to leave. She was no longer the Southern belle in pink and lace. She wore jeans and a shirt, just like a man. Random nodded appreciatively. This was another side of a girl he'd thought of at first as a fragile, sheltered beauty.

"Good afternoon, Mr. Random."

"Good afternoon. Going riding?"

"Why, yes," Junella said. She noticed the way he was looking at her and blushed. "I suppose you're thinking it's quite improper of me to go riding this way. I ought to be all decked out like I was earlier and have myself a nice, lady-like sidesaddle."

Random smiled. "I would have expected it, yes. But it's not for me to say what's proper and what is not, is it?"

"Well, you have to remember I'm a Texas girl," she said. "All that fanciness is for Eastern ladies. Would you be too embarrassed to be seen accompanying a lady riding astride? I was going to head up to the high pasture. Red—my horse—needs some exercise."

"Considering the trouble you went to in my behalf this morning," Random said with a gentle smile, "I'll compromise my principles enough to be seen in public with you. If anyone looks our way, I'll cover my face with my hat."

The wooded hills between San Rael and the southern pastures were cool and dappled green. Random and Junella rode side by side, Random's little gray dwarfed by the high-stepping red gelding. Mountain jays squabbled raucously overhead.

"I'm sorry your uncle had to rouse himself for the meeting, Junella," Random said. "I know he's feeling bad."

Junella shook her head. "Uncle Clay insisted. He said he wanted to keep Mr. Carroll on a checkrein, so he wouldn't talk the others around to his point of view. I think Mr. Carroll would a lot rather have Cal Sharper doing the job you're doing, Mr. Random."

"Carroll lost a lot of money when the railroad deal fell through?"

"Why, how did you know that?"

"Just say I guessed it."

Junella turned to face straight ahead. "Well, you can't really blame him, can you? I don't know what Uncle Clay is thinking about. A man in his condition, doing the things he's doing—and all to save a bunch of uppity Mexicans! I can't understand."

Random looked sidelong at her. Her profile was pert and fetching, but at the moment it was drawn into grim lines. He sighed mentally and gave up the idea of trying to explain the matter to her. "Would you rather Cal Sharper *was* doing my job, Junella?" he asked softly.

She colored. "I don't care for that Sharper boy one bit, Mr. Random," she said. "He's gotten fresh with me before, and I put him in his place real sharply." She turned back to Random. "But he's got the right idea of how to deal with the greasers, Mr. Random. The gun and the rope's all those people understand."

The contempt in her voice took him aback. She was a lovely girl, an intelligent girl. But her hate was like a dark curtain between them.

"With luck your uncle won't have to trouble himself much longer."

Junella glanced at her companion sharply. "Why, what do you mean?"

He almost told her, then checked himself. Gonzalez
had said that one of the *gorras* had grown disillusioned with *El Jefe* and his night-riding bravos after
the Cranston murder. Approached properly, the man
could very well supply the key to the problem. However, the man's identity would have to be kept secret.
And, while Random trusted the girl, he did not think
it was advisable to noise it around that the *gorras* had
a turncoat in their ranks.

"I think I may be able to set a trap for our elusive
Noe Villareal," he said to her.

The girl looked puzzled at this. Her attention was
distracted by a gray squirrel who perched on a pine
bough over the trail, bitterly and vocally resenting
their intrusion. When they rode beneath him, he
bombarded them with pine cones. One of the missiles
scored a direct hit on the crown of Random's battered black felt hat. The young riders thought this
was hilariously funny, and after their laughter had
subsided, no more was said of Clay Barnes or the
night riders.

The Ponderosa pines thinned and the land opened
up before them into a rolling meadow. The grass was
yellow, but the spring runoff had dusted the hills
with pale green shoots. The cattle were grazing contentedly on the sweet spring growth, black dots scattered in handfuls over the grassland.

"I'll race you!" Junella suddenly cried as they came
out on level ground. "That dead tree over there. Let's
go!" She booted the big gelding and they were off.

Random grinned. The red's long-legged stride was
eating up the ground between him and the lightning-
blasted tree that stood by itself five hundred yards
away. Weather had bleached the tree so that it looked
like a broken bone sticking out of the earth. The
blue-coated youth touched his spurs to the little
mare's sides and bent over, pouring soft syllables into
her ears like honey.

Halfway to the corpse of the tree, the gray roan

went by the huge gelding, her neck arched and her head tucked back. Random's lengthy coattails flapped behind him in the breeze. The plucky mare made the tree well ahead of the red horse, and Random took the animal once around the tree almost on her side before slowing her to a walk.

Laughing, Junella reined in to a walk as she arrived. "You win, Mr. Random!" she called. "Red's reckoned a good runner hereabouts, but that little mare of yours goes like the wind. What's your secret."

Random stopped the gray and slapped her affectionately on the neck. She was barely breathing hard, though the big red was blowing with exertion. "I talk to her, that's all."

"I talk to Red, too," Junella said.

"Ah, but that's my secret," Random laughed. "This little lady is part Arabian and I speak to her in Arabic. You said she goes like the wind, and well she might. *Bint al-Rih,* I call her. Daughter of the wind."

"How poetic!" Junella studied him for a moment. "I wouldn't have picked you for a horse like her. You look more like the type for a Tennessee Walker or something. Just something about you."

"No," he said. "When I was in Algeria, I saw how the native horses could keep going when the big handsome chargers of the French officers were dropping from thirst and exhaustion. When I got to this country I knew I was coming West, so I looked for an Arabian horse. They're bred for this type of country. And for war."

"Really? That sounds so exciting," Junella said. "Tell me about Arabia, Mr. Random."

"It's vast, roughly triangular in shape, and I've never laid eyes on it in my life."

"You're making fun of me, sir. You say you speak Arabic. Were you really never in Arabia?"

"They speak a dialect of Arabic in Algeria, where I was."

"Oh," Junella said. They were walking their horses

easily over the rolling pastureland now. "How did you come to be in the French Foreign Legion, Mr. Random?"

"In *la Légion,* it's poor form to ask such a question," Random said. Junella's cheeks colored. "There, don't apologize! I meant no criticism. I only meant that, strange as it seems, I have never been asked that before."

"Well, you're an American, aren't you?" He nodded. "I wondered how you happened to be in Africa—it's so *far.*" Her eyes were distant as she tried to envision how far Africa was.

Random rode a ways in silence. "I took quite a roundabout route. When I left the States, I was young—nine years old, as I recall—and I became a cabin boy on a freighter. A drunken mate ran us aground in a North Sea storm. Only six of us survived, out of a crew of thirty. We were rescued by a ship bound for Hamburg, and that's where I landed, after three years at sea."

"Where is Hamburg?"

"On the Elbe river, in the north of Germany. I grew up on the docks of Hamburg. It was a rough, grimy, often brutal existence, but the lessons I learned there have helped me time and again to survive."

Junella was gazing at him, wide-eyed. She had never in her life laid eyes on an ocean. And what she knew of waterfront towns reminded her of border towns—both were dirty, dangerous places, hardly suitable for a young child to grow up in. Random noticed the way she was looking at him, and smiled to himself. He knew what she was thinking. He also knew the grim reality of his adolescent years was far worse than anything the girl could imagine.

"That period of my life ended with a misunderstanding with a harbor policeman. He was a brutal swine who liked to beat his prisoners with a lead-

tipped cudgel. However, he *was* a policeman, and because he died, I had to leave Hamburg in a hurry."

Random remembered Ajaccio, the squat, hook-
nosed Corsican with the knife-scarred face. He had
been one of Random's mentors, one of those who had
befriended the skinny foreign boy, taught him how to
stay alive in the alleys and on the docks. *Hold the
blade low, and keep the point up,* the Corsican had
said, demonstrating with his own slim stiletto. *If you
want the heart, go through the belly, so the rib cage
won't turn your point. Only an* imbécile *tries to
thrust his blade through bone.*

Random had learned that lesson well. He could
still recall the peculiar feeling, the soft sound, as his
knife slid into the belly of the harbor patrolman. The
man's pig eyes rolled up, his knees gave way, and he
died. Whether Junella Barnes believed it or not, it was
the first time Random had killed, and it still made
him cold to think of it.

"I headed south," the young man continued,
"hoping to find sanctuary. I was hounded through
Germany by officers with orders to kill me on sight—
Hamburg isn't part of the Empire, but they had some
kind of police agreement. I had some close scrapes
and made it across the frontier into France with the
wolf pack at my heels. Once in France I sought the
best refuge I could find—the Legion, and North Africa."

"How old were you when this happened?" the girl
asked dubiously.

"The Legion requires its recruits to be at least
eighteen years of age," Random replied. "Of course,
they had no way of checking my age, and I stood well
over six feet at the time. And they're always in need
of men to die for *la gloire,* so it didn't matter much
that I was two years shy of the minimum age."

"You were *sixteen?*"

"Yes. It was a hard life, but after the docks it
wasn't too difficult to get used to."

Junella shook her head skeptically. It all sounded so outlandish. But at the same time, Random was so matter-of-fact it was hard to believe he was spinning her the whole cloth. "You haven't really answered my question, Mr. Random," she said. "Why did you leave this country in the first place?"

Random rubbed at the mark on his left cheek. "Miss Barnes," he said, "You quite obviously think I'm either lying or having a joke at your expense, and you're too well brought-up a young lady to say so outright. So, rather than having me give you an answer you won't believe either, why not let your imagination create a fitting beginning to my story? It would probably sound less unlikely than the truth."

"You say that very prettily," Junella laughed. "All right. I won't ask any more questions about your dark and mysterious past. And I guess you're right, I do have trouble believing the things you've told me. I have trouble even believing there are really places like Arabia or Algeria."

"Do you know what fascinates the Legionnaires?" Random asked. On a distant hill a rider waved to them in greeting, then rode off as they returned the gesture. They had been seeing riders since arriving at the high pasture, but none of them ever got close. It struck Random as odd. But with such an attractive and attentive companion he had other things on his mind.

"What?" the girl asked.

"Here." A sweep of his arm took in the horizons. "The West. All Europeans seem to be mad for cowboys and Indians and all the rest. More Frenchmen know the names of Crazy Horse and Custer than of their own prime minister."

Junella was delighted. "Really?" she said. "That's amazing. I mean, there's nothing exciting about cowboys, and Indians are scary and dirty." Random remembered how she had come to be living in San Rael. "But there's not anything unusual about them."

"Not to you," Random grinned. "But veiled women and robed Bedouin warriors and braying camels are nothing out of the ordinary in North Africa. It's all a matter of where you are, and what you're used to."

Junella mulled this over. Random looked toward the spiny hunch of mountains to the west. They were outlined with sunset colors. He pulled his watch from a pocket of his coat. "I'd best get you home, Miss Barnes," he said. "It's close to suppertime, and your uncle will be upset if you're late."

"I've had the most delightful time, Mr. Random," Junella said. "You'll stay on for supper, won't you?"

"Gladly, thank you."

"Good," she said. "Uncle Clay likes to hear your stories as much as I do. Race you home!" She turned the red and touched him with her spurs.

Out of courtesy Random let his hostess beat him back to the white mansion on the hillside, but he missed dining at the Barnes's table that evening. When the lathered horses pulled up in front of the house and the pair dismounted, pink-cheeked and cheerful from the ride, the stable hand came out to take the animals and cool them off. He was a shy boy of twelve or thirteen named Gavin, a neighbor boy. Junella sprang, still laughing, up the steps to the door. The boy plucked timidly at Random's sleeve before he could follow.

"Mr. Random, sir?" he said, eyes big. "There's a man to see you, sir, out behind the barn, near the woods. Says it can't wait."

Random smiled at the towheaded youngster. "He'll have to, Gavin," he said. "Miss Junella expects my company for dinner."

The boy looked stricken. "B-but he said you'd want to see him right away. Said you'd know what about." He stopped and looked around, then spoke in a conspiratorial whisper. "He's a Meskin, sir. Says a Seenyor Gon-zolles sent him to you."

Random stopped short on the steps. "Oh," he said lamely. "Thank you." He came back down and took the horses' reins. "I'll tend to these. You run in and give Miss Junella my regrets. Tell her I have urgent business to attend to. She'll understand."

The boy dashed up onto the porch and knocked on the door. He was proud enough to burst that the glamorous stranger had entrusted him with this mission. He was struck by hero worship, which Random, not that much older himself, would not have come within a country mile of realizing.

A man sat in the lee of the barn, all but hidden in the shadows. He stood up nervously when Random stepped around a corner of the barn. "Señor Random?" he said. He was a youngish *nativo*, perhaps seven years older than Random, and fairly handsome.

"Yes. What can I do for you, señor?" Random managed to keep the excitement he felt from creeping into his voice.

"I am José Pacheco. Eulógio Gonzalez sent me."

Random offered his hand. Hesitantly the man shook it. Then he stepped back gingerly.

He glanced around as Gavin had done, to make sure no one was watching. Satisfied, he turned back to the taller man.

"I am a *gorra blanca,* señor," he said.

CHAPTER NINE

The room was full of alcohol fumes and the wet-wool smell of old men. Agitated Spanish buzzed like a swarm of bees around the firelit *vigas*. The *viejos* all talked at once. Some of them glared at their portly host with rheumy malevolence.

"An Anglo!"—"A *gringo*! You want us to listen to a *gringo*?"—"Eulógio, you are *loco*!"

Patiently Gonzalez sat out the storm of protest. At last he spread his hands like oil on the water and the babble subsided. "You know me, my friends," he said. "You know you can trust me, *qué no*?"

"*Sí*, we trust you, but anyone can go out of his head. My great-uncle Seferino—"

"I am not out of my head, Crístobal Ramirez. I am doing a thing that is very hard for me, but I believe it to be the only thing to do. Señor Random?"

A door opened and Random came in. He had just spoken with Elena. Her long patrician face had been strained and her voice was brisk. She had welcomed him in very formal English, and then had stood staring at him.

"My father," she'd finally said. "Take care of him, please. I know what you are asking of him." She turned and left the room quickly, so that Random would not see her composure break. The encounter had drained Random. He was endangering both Elena and her father. But he had a job to do, and this was the only way to do it.

He had tried to tell himself that they were in danger anyway. Had not Gonzalez been in deadly danger that very first time Random had met him? But it didn't work. Random knew how groups like the night riders treated those they regarded as traitors in their midst, and they would certainly believe the Gonzalezes were betraying them, if they found out what was going on.

Twenty pairs of aged dark eyes fastened on him as he entered the *sala*. Hostility washed over him. He stood and let the *viejos* look him over all they wanted. He turned his head to meet an angry gaze here and there with frank green eyes. Gonzalez introduced him in Spanish.

"Isn't he the one the *gringos* have hired? The soldier of fortune?"

"He is," Gonzalez replied.

"Ay, you have gone *loco*!" old Crístobal Ramirez declared. "Why did you bring us here? So the *gringo* gunfighter can get a good look at us?"

"Listen to me!" It was the first time Random, or for that matter most of the men in the room, had heard Eulógio Gonzalez raise his voice. "The *gorras blancas* are destroying the friendship we have always had with our Anglo neighbors. They are drawing us into a war with our Anglo neighbors. A war we can never win, my friends. We must stop them."

"But what good will it do us to bring this *chota* in on it?"

"He saved my life," Gonzalez said. "From four Anglos. Do you still think he is a goat?" Quietly he told the story of how Random had rescued him.

"Señor Random swears that his only goal is to stop the night riding of the *gorras blancas*. I called you here because I felt you would realize we need this done as badly as the Anglos. And he says he needs our help." Gonzalez shrugged. "I believe him. I trust him because he saved my life, *sí*. But I also believe him because what he says is true. You are old men and wise—listen to his wisdom."

He nodded to the tall young Anglo. Random cleared his throat and spoke. "The *gorras* claim to be fighting for the rights and dignity of your people," he said. "What rights have they won you? Does burning barns and destroying the livelihoods of your old neighbors win you rights? Does killing in cold blood a man who was a friend to all *nativos* in spite of his white skin earn you dignity? You know better." He paused for Gonzalez to translate. The flickering firelight made his face all angles and planes. His eyes were shadowed, like the eyes of a hawk.

"Some of the Anglos hate you," Random went on. "Some resent you for not selling your homes to the railroad company. This is no concern of mine. I think they are wrong, and I have told them this."

The *viejos* were disbelieving. "When does a lackey talk back to his master?" one demanded.

"I am a professional soldier," Random said. "I am not a gunfighter. The Anglos hired me because they saw no other way to stop the raids. There were those who wanted to take their revenge on you all for the acts of the White Hoods, but the wiser ones had their way. And I am a specialist. One does not tell a doctor how to diagnose one's illness, if one wants to be cured. They do not tell me my business. Still, if I cannot stop the raids soon, the ones who hate you will prevail, and there will be war. That is why you must help me."

"Help you against the *gorras*? Never!"

"Then I will fail. And Cal Sharper and the other hotheaded Anglo youths will ride into your town, to teach you a lesson, as they would say. Why let this happen? Is it not enough that some Anglos hate you? Do you want them all to?"

The argument Random's questions provoked were vehement. Random leaned against a crowded bookshelf and tried to puzzle out which way the conversation was going from his still rudimentary command of the Spanish tongue. Finally Ramirez spoke to him.

"We do not like the *gorras*," the withered oldster said by way of Gonzalez. "They are disrespectful. They take what they want and tell us we should be glad to aid them. And you are right that they might cause all the Anglos to hate us. But why should we help you?"

"I ask very little. Just refuse to aid the *gorras* when they ask it."

"They'd kill us!" piped a frail voice.

"Then are they truly fighting for you? How many *viejos* have the Anglos killed?"

"The Anglos are still trying to run us off!" another ancient boomed. Despite his obvious age he was big and powerful-looking. Incongruously blue eyes shone brightly from his dark face, above a huge patriarchal white beard. This was Juan Romero, Gonzalez said. He owned land directly in the path of the proposed railway. "They have challenged our right to own our land, in the county court at Los Duranes! Why should we help them? The *gorras* are evil, but why should we help our enemies rob us?"

The room swam in Random's vision. If this was so his whole strategy was worthless. He'd thought killing *El Jefe* would solve everything. But if such a suit had been filed the raids would go on with or without the white-hooded leader. "Do you know this to be true?"

"I have heard it. *El Jefe* has shown the young men papers. In early summer the court will decide whether we own the land." The burly old man spat. "Whether we own the land we grew up on, and our fathers before us for generations!"

Feeling sick, Random looked the fierce old man straight in the eye. "I will speak to my employers about this," he said slowly. "If it is true, they will withdraw the suit at once. If they refuse—" He looked around the room. "If they refuse I shall return their money and ride out of San Rael, and I will never return. I swear this on my honor as a gentleman." He folded his arms and stood as Gonzalez translated, trying not to show the turmoil within. *This changes everything,* he thought. *How much can I salvage?*

A seemingly endless wrangle ensued. Could they trust the strange green-eyed *gringo* soldier? There was fire in him, and steel, anyone could see that. Eulógio Gonzalez, whom all knew and respected as a just, wise man, vouched for him without reservation.

But who could trust a *gringo*? A hired killer?

What kind of hired killer saved an enemy from the people who had hired him? No, the *gringo* was telling the truth.

Then he was crazy, insisted some.

"Yes, very well. Random was *loco*. But what of that? He spoke the truth. The *gorras* would bring ruin on them all. The night riders were not saviors of their people. They rode for themselves, for the joy of raiding and terrorizing.

In the end it was the romanticism that ran so deeply through all Latins—the French as well as the Spanish, as Random could attest—that swung the *viejos* in the young outsider's favor. It was the same thing that made the young *nativos* eager to follow a mysterious leader who hid in the daytime and never permitted his face to be seen, even by his most trusted lieutenants. There was dash and daring in Random, in his style, and the old men liked that.

Juan Romero spoke for the group, standing straight and tall as a Biblical prophet. "If you say so, Eulógio, we will accept the Anglo as a man of honor. As men of honor, we can do no less than trust him—for the time."

He paused. "No longer will we permit the *gorras* to ride across our lands on their way to raids. No longer will we feed and shelter them. But the challenge against us must be withdrawn. If it is not, we shall give the White Hoods any help they need to fight the Anglos. And let come what may. On this, we give *our* word of honor!"

*   *   *

"God damn it, what fool is suing to have the natives thrown off their lands?" Random burst like a bomb on the tranquil gathering in Clay Barnes's parlor. "I will not have it!"

His employers, already seated and enjoying a few forenoon drinks, stared at him as if he'd stormed in wearing war paint and feathers. Lacey was at his elbow, trying to get him to surrender his hat and long coat.

"What are you talking about?" Dr. Stern asked.

Random stood, eyeing the group narrowly. He stared at each man in turn, but all he got back was blank looks. "What do you mean?" he asked suspiciously.

"What's all this crap about a suit?" Carroll asked bluntly.

Random glared at him. "If anyone knows anything about it, you do," he said. "Someone from this town has filed suit in Los Duranes to have the Mexicans' ownership of their own land voided. Does that sound familiar?"

The men exchanged baffled looks. "No, it doesn't," Bacon said timorously.

"I don't believe anyone here knows anything about it," Barnes said.

"You mean none of you filed the suit?"

"No sir," Tanner said, "we surely did not."

Random dropped heavily into a chair. "For your sakes, gentlemen, I hope to Christ that's true. Because if it's not, one of you has done the stupidest damned thing he possibly could."

"Please explain yourself, sir," the doctor requested.

"With pleasure. If someone really is trying to steal the natives' land, by what passes for legal means, the war has already begun. The natives will be convinced *El Jefe* and his night-riding cutthroats are right. They'll turn against you to the last man. I spoke to some of their old men last night. They don't like the *gorras*. They're afraid of them. But they're more afraid of you, because of this insane lawsuit!"

"What do you want from a bunch of old greasers?" Bacon asked.

"Help. The *gorras* are young men, early twenties for the most part. The older men resent the youngsters to begin with. And without help from the native community, the *gorras blancas* may as well close up shop. They can't live without that support any more than a fish can live out of water."

"Now, wait a minute," Hoopwright said. "I thought you was going to kill this Villareal. Said it would take the steam out of the Mexes. What happened to that idea?"

"It won't work any more," Random said bitterly. "Don't you see that? Whether this suit is real or not the damage is done. Fear will keep the *gorras* riding even with *El Jefe* dead. Someone's stupid greed has ruined the only plan that had a chance of working!"

"Well, who the hell are you to take that tone of voice with us, boy?" Carroll demanded angrily. He had come out of his shock at the young man's outburst enough to resume his customary truculence. "We're payin' you, boy. You're just a hired hand."

"I am not being paid to risk my life to cover the mistakes of a pack of idiots!" Random said stonily. "I accept the risk of dying as part of the job, but I will not die for your greed and stupidity."

"You can't talk to me that way!" roared Carroll, coming out of his easy chair.

"Go ahead and fire me then!" Random shouted back. "Have yourselves a bloodbath, by all means! I won't be a part of it!"

Carroll was burly but shorter than the mercenary. No one in the room doubted the lean outsider could handle himself with deadly skill. Tanner clamped a heavy hand on the rancher's shoulder and pulled him back in his chair. Carroll sat with his mouth working like a carp's.

"You're not so all fired hot!" he choked out at last. "You went and got yourself cut up over in Africa, if that story in Clay's magazine ain't a line of bull."

Random was on his feet in a second, face white with fury. He was out of his swallow-tailed coat and tearing open his shirt before anybody could move or speak.

"Line of bull?" he snapped. "Here, damn you, see for youself!"

Buttons flew all over the room as Random bared his chest. "Jesus Christ," someone breathed.

The youth had a hole in his chest, a quarter-sized depression two inches below his left nipple. A scarlet line radiated off to the left, trailing back across the rib cage under his arm. Sweat stood out on Random's forehead. His perforated chest worked like a bellows.

Dr. Stern peered at him with professional interest. "You're a very lucky young man," he said. "A quarter inch higher, or any farther to the right, and you would not be standing here."

"Call it luck if you will," Random said. "It felt like death when it happened. It should have killed me. And it happened because I was trying to cover for someone else's stupidity. In those days I was under military discipline and had no choice but to stand up and let myself get stuck like a pig. I'm not now. You're paying me, but you can have every cent of your money back if you think I'll cover your mistakes. Go ahead and try to run out your neighbors. Let Sharper and his friends shoot holes in every brown hide they see. I will not be involved!"

He spun away from them and stood with his arms folded across his chest. The townsmen exchanged stunned looks.

"You done all right by us so far," Tanner said slowly. "You still think those patrols are gonna work, or is everything changed around so they won't no more?"

Random shrugged. "They should keep the raiders at bay for now."

"Well now, I'm sure you can figger out something to put a stop to these raids even if this lawsuit deal has throwed all your plans out the window." He settled back in his chair.

"I reckon I don't cotton to a man takin' the tone with me you did a while back any more than Tag does, but I think maybe you've earned the right." He looked sharply at Carroll. "We brung you here to do a job for us, Mr. Random, and some of us ain't been backing you like we should. Far as I'm concerned, you keep working for us, we'll do things your way."

Random nodded, buttoned the surviving buttons of his shirt, and left without another word.

Random did keep working. Despite the radical change in the situation he saw no reason to take the pressure off the raiders. He had to change his long-range plans, but even as he racked his brains for a new strategy, he kept up the defense of San Rael and his attempts to undermine the night riders' morale.

The next three nights the *gorras* struck in spite of the growing moonlight. Each time, Random's men, warned by watchers hidden beside the trails, met the White Hoods and drove them off. There were no further casualties to either side. Random's prediction proved correct: The marauders had no stomach for battle.

Repercussions were soon felt. Cal Sharper all but disappeared from sight. He and his friends, particularly Jerry Moody, who'd wanted to draw on Russ Gorman in the *cantina* the day Shorty had been killed—and whom Random had belatedly recognized as the third of the masked riders who'd tried to murder Eulógio Gonzalez—were occasionally seen clumped in dark corners of Turk's muttering that someone ought to teach Random a lesson. Random's riders had become his almost fanatical supporters. The rest of the Anglo settlers were coming over to the same point of view. Random was doing his job well beyond any expectation.

Among the *nativos* things were changing as well. The *gorras* were finding it harder and harder to get any cooperation at all. More natives forbade them to cross their lands every day.

One night three masked men appeared at the door of old Juan Romero's *casa* demanding to know why he was betraying the *gorras,* the heroic champions of his people. He opened fire on them with a shotgun and sent the hooded heroes fleeing into the darkness.

And the morning after each failed raid Random rode into the native village to drink at the pink *cantina.* Young *nativos* were always there, hot-eyed and sullen, speaking muffled, bitter Spanish. They answered Random's courteous greetings with scowls. But no one challenged him.

Afternoons Random rode to visit Señor Gonzalez and his daughter. He needed something to take his mind off the seemingly insoluble problem of how to put a final end to the *gorras'* terror without touching off a race war. He made and discarded dozens of plans, each less practical than the last. The Gonzalez house was a cool refuge.

Elena Gonzalez was reserved but polite. Random knew she was wary of him. He also suspected that she cared more than she would admit for the impetuous Roberto Morales, and was afraid he'd come to harm riding with the *gorras.*

The time was passed by Random learning Spanish and telling stories of the things and places he'd seen. He sympathized with the plump, heavily moustached Gonzalez. The older man was an intellectual who loved books and learned talk. Educated at the university in Mexico City, he had found no place for himself in that lofty institution. Down there he was regarded as a provincial, little better than the pale-skinned barbarians he had been raised among in New

Mexico. And the North American colleges weren't welcoming any Mexicans with open arms. So he had settled in resignedly to ranching his family's land in Duran County, raising cattle and alfalfa and fathering a lovely strong-willed daughter.

Random was something of an intellectual himself. The circumstances of his life had turned him into a man of action. His desire for learning had been satisfied largely by the study of languages and weighty books of military history, theory, strategy. His problem was, having once tasted the excitement and adventure of an active, daring life, he was addicted. He could never give up the stimulation danger gave him for the paler sensations of the library of a college campus. That was why he had become a mercenary. He didn't need the money. It was the blood rush of combat he required to survive.

The only man who truly understood this need of his was one who shared it. After Little Big Horn Russ Gorman had left the Army a disgusted, disillusioned man. He returned to San Rael and tried his hand at farming. But he was no more a farmer than Random was a university don. He was ridden by the need to be doing something more than scratching in the dirt and growing old in a mountain backwater. Unlike Random, however, he had found no outlet for his dissatisfaction. Until the young outsider had arrived to lead the fight against *las gorras blancas*.

Since the night the ex-scout had saved Random's life the two had become close friends. There was more to their relationship than the mere fact that Random owed the other a life. Despite the difference in age and background, the harsh experiences of their lives had given them much in common. Random had seen the grimness of war in North Africa, the revolt of 1880–81 and its brutal suppression. Gorman had been through the Indian wars of the American West. From the time as a young trooper he had been with the first regular army units to come upon the grisly

remains of the Sand Creek Massacre by John Chivington and the Third Colorado Volunteer Cavalry,
through the Custer campaigns, the treacherous American attack at the Washita, to the terrible culmina-
tion of Little Big Horn, he had seen the worst one
human being could work upon another.

The man possessed a depth of compassion seldom
found in one of his hard physical competence. He
was in his way a zealot, a hater of brutality and the
brutal. Random came to understand that he loathed
the *gorras* for the same reasons Señor Gonzales did—
but also that, had Random showed himself to be cut
from the same cloth as Cal Sharper, the blue-coated
youth would have left his bones on the Morris ranch.
Gorman had said as much, and once Random found
he'd meant it, his respect for his lieutenant went up a
great deal.

And all the time Random wondered how to finish
this business he'd begun.

He might have recalled the lesson he'd learned on
the North Sea, however: If winds can blow foul without warning, they can turn fair just as suddenly.

On the morning after the fourth unsuccessful night
raid since Random's arrival, he had a visitor in the
early hours at his schoolhouse headquarters. It was
José Pacheco, and the man was excited.

There was to be a meeting that night. For the first
time since Luke Cranston's death *El Jefe* would show
himself. Random's breath seemed hard to catch as he
listened to the *nativo*.

He knew now what must be done.

CHAPTER TEN

Dinner for Random that night was good roast beef at Clay Barnes's table. Random felt no guilt at dining in such splendor, since his men were free to eat in their own homes whatever fare they were accustomed to. Had they been on patrol with the Legion in the blistering desert, with thin gruel and blood sausage to sustain them, he would have felt differently.

The company was as good as the food. Clay Barnes's back seemed to be troubling him less, though he had come to dinner with the aid of a cane. Junella was a vision in pale green silk, and the candlelight made her sky-blue eyes seem twice as large.

The occasion even caused Random to relax his self-imposed prohibition against drinking while working. Barnes had a wine served which, he said, he hoped would not offend Random's French-trained palate. Random laughed at this; the palate of a Legionnaire was more accustomed to concoctions well suited to unclogging drainpipes or removing paint than to fine wines. But he had learned enough to recognize that what his host served ranked with the finest.

The wine, or perhaps the wholly unanticipated possibility of quick success, made Random loosen his reserve. As Lacey gathered up the gravy-stained dishes and bustled them off to the kitchen, Random sat back and offered a toast to what could be, if all went well, the last night of the *gorras blancas* in Duran County.

He drank with Barnes and his ward, then held up

his glass and watched candlelight sparkle in the red liquid. *How like blood it looks,* he thought.

If all did *not* go well this could be his last night to savor such pleasures.

"There is no guarantee that I will succeed tonight," he said. "But I have a certain advantage. *El Jefe* will feel safe as a lion in his own lair. I may be able to cut the heart out of the raiders tonight."

"Are you going to kill him?" Junella asked. Random hoped it was the light of the candles that caused the glitter in her pretty eyes.

"No," he said. He tried to explain how the lawsuit had been the joker. If not for it, then, indeed, killing Villareal would in effect kill the White Hoods.

But it wasn't that simple. Convinced the Anglos were challenging their very right to their own lands, the *nativos* would have fear to hold them together as *El Jefe*'s personality and quicksilver tongue had done. And Villareal would still lead them—as a martyred victim of *gringo* treachery.

A dead Villareal was no good to Random. But a live one could be helpful indeed. If Random could capture him tonight, in the very center of his power, he would lose face—for a charismatic leader, humiliation was more damaging than death. And Random was fairly sure that, once *El Jefe* was in custody, a way could be found to discredit him and his cause.

His explanations met with skepticism. Junella seemed to think shooting Villareal was still a fine idea, and who cared what the Mexicans thought? Barnes's objections were more on the practical side.

"That's a tall order, son," he said. "You'll be on your own. How exactly do you plan on catching him?"

Random smiled ruefully. "I don't know exactly," he admitted frankly. "All I know about what will happen tonight is what my informant could tell me, and it wasn't enough to make detailed plans. I couldn't even reconnoiter the area in advance—a

white face is too conspicuous, and at the first sign an
Anglo knows what's going on Villareal will dive back
down his deep dark hole."

He set the wine glass down. "It's like a hunter going after a wounded cat," he said. "It's shrewd, wary
game, and the hunter can count on just one chance
at it."

"It sounds impossible," Junella said.

"It could be. But look: Villareal won't be expecting
trouble. He has guards, but they're mostly for show. I
think I can create some kind of stir and separate him
from the rest." He brushed hair from his eyes. "I've
done this sort of thing before. It's risky, but it can be
done."

Junella looked concerned. "Be careful."

"I will."

At the crest of the hill overlooking the Barnes
house, Random paused. Everything was in place, the
long rifle in the boot, the shotgun in a pocket of his
long coat, heavy binoculars hanging from his neck by
a strap. He checked his watch by the gleam of the
gibbous moon pushing up over the eastern peaks. Satisfied, he made a low clucking sound with his tongue.
Shortly he heard it returned, and a second horseman
joined him on the hilltop.

"*Buenas noches,*" José Pacheco said. His teeth
flashed in his dark face. Random nodded a reply and
they set off.

The two circled through the wooded hills south of
San Rael. They crossed the Trail well to the west of
town and headed north toward the Mexican settlement. On the way Pacheco reached inside his sheep-
skin jacket and brought out a piece of cloth. It
glowed greenish white in the moonlight. A white
hood, with holes for the eyes: a *gorra blanca.*

"Not yet," Random whispered. "It's too likely to be
seen. And if an Anglo sees it, he's apt to start shoot-

ing." Pacheco grunted and nodded, stuffing the hood back into his pocket.

To reach the meeting place of the night riders, the pair would have to pass by Random's own pickets. He did not expect much trouble from them, though. Even though he had not told his men, other than Gorman, what he intended to do tonight, they would be looking for traffic heading away from the native village, not toward it. And a couple of riders could take trails smaller than the ones the *gorra* parties had to follow.

After the first raid was turned back, Random was afraid *El Jefe* would take the risk of breaking the raiding parties up and trying to infiltrate the White Hoods singly and in pairs. It would have been chancy, but had it worked, it would have canceled Random's defensive measures.

Now it was too late. The *gorras* were running scared. *El Jefe* did not dare split his raiding parties.

Quietly Random and Pacheco approached the trail through the forest, the westernmost path under Random's surveillance. They passed to the south of where two Anglos waited in covert for the hooded marauders. As Random had expected, the sentries' eyes were fixed uptrail, toward the *nativo* village, but there were a few heart-pounding minutes as the riders slipped by. Men on patrol would be apt to be trigger happy from the tension of constant alertness.

Random and the renegade *gorra* crossed the trail without incident and were on their way. The young soldier of fortune breathed a sigh of relief.

Gorman, of course, had protested when he learned that Random was going to be taking on the whole lot of night riders single-handedly. "You can't handle this alone!" he'd objected. "You're damned good, but this is throwing your life away and you know it!"

Random had looked at him steadily in the fading daylight. "This could be our only chance at Villareal, *mon ami,*" he'd said. "He hasn't accompanied any of the raiding parties we've turned back. Damn it, he's the key to this whole stinking mess. Even if I don't capture him I can scare him, shake his followers' confidence in him. If we miss him now how are we going to find him again? I take an army and I'll never even set eyes on him."

Gorman had set his jaw with bulldog Black Irish tenacity. "Even if just the two of us go, that doubles the chance we'll be discovered," Random said. "And if I do get caught, and maybe stop a ball from a Walker Colt? I need you here, alive, to take over if something happens to me. Or would you rather see Cal Sharper take over where I left off?"

His friend's face had clouded. Then the thunderheads parted and Gorman flashed a warm, lopsided grin at the younger man. "Well, if that's to be the way of it, good luck," he'd said. A thick hand clapped Random's shoulder, and Gorman's parting handshake had been firm.

Right now, Random knew, the former cavalryman would be feigning sleep back at the schoolhouse, waiting for the sound of gunfire.

With the dimly seen form of Pacheco in the lead, they skirted the huddle of the Mexican village. They passed within a hundred yards of a boxy little house from which a dog ran barking a challenge. Random froze, remembering what Gonzalez had told him about the *nativo* dogs. When they smelled a stranger they set up a clamor that spread through the night like a prairie blaze, till the whole countryside knew intruders were about. But Pacheco spoke to the mongrel in Spanish and it trotted up wagging its tail. He leaned down to pat its furry head. Tongue lolling, the dog went off into the darkness. The riders were not troubled again by canine sentries.

The meeting place of the *gorras blancas* was a sheltered clearing about three and a half miles northeast of the village. One minute there was nothing ahead but black forest; the next they came over a hill to find a hundred-yard wide bowl opening before them. The bowl was filled with light and moving shapes.

Pacheco touched Random's arm. Drifting back down the slope, they circled the clearing. Now that he was listening, Random could hear the snorting and pawing of the horses and subdued murmur from the men.

The native showed Random an outcrop of rock perched on the very lip of the bowl. A man could wriggle into the tangle of rocks and be completely lost to view, even in the light of day. By peering through a clump of scrub cedar, he could see everything that took place in the depression. When he had seen the place, Random and Pacheco rode off a ways to a stand of young pines. Random tied the mare, nose muffled in a rag. He took the rifle from its scabbard.

"I must go," Pacheco said. He took out his hood and pulled it on. It made him look like a ghost. "It is up to you. Good luck, *amigo*." He wheeled the sorrel and was gone, so softly Random could scarcely hear him go.

Walking carefully on a carpet of fallen pine needles, Random made his way back to the rocks. He slid the rifle in, then slithered after it. It was a close fit, but by bending at the waist his whole lanky body would fit in the enclosed space. He wriggled forward on his belly, holding the binoculars up off the rock. Gingerly, he parted the bushes and peered out.

The light in the hollow came from a score of torches. Even as the unseen watcher looked on, several hooded men stooped over a pile of wood and brush, lighting it from a torch they carried. The bonfire flared. Red-lit, fragrant smoke climbed toward the stars.

Random let his breath out between his teeth in a soundless whistle. *Look at them!* he said to himself. *Forty, maybe fifty*. Pacheco appeared on the edge of the clearing. His sorrel whickered and sidestepped at the commotion. He dismounted as Random did some mental figuring.

According to Mrs. Vardeman's book, the *nativo* population of San Rael was around two hundred fifty in 1878. In the last five years it would not have grown much. At a reasonable guess, half the young Mexican men must be here!

The hooded men milled around. They spoke in voices muffled by their *gorras*. It was obvious that their leader had not yet arrived. They must still be confident on their own grounds, Random thought, since they had put no pickets out to guard the meeting. Or perhaps they were there, but inattentive enough to miss Random and Pacheco sneaking in. And why not? The Anglos had made no overt move against them. And what Anglo in his right mind would be wandering these woods at night with the White Hoods still active?

Shrouded heads turned. Suddenly *El Jefe* was there. He loomed up out of the night on an immense blaze-faced black stallion whose glossy hide gleamed like oiled silk in the torchlight. Four hooded attendants flanked him on horseback. Random grinned appreciatively. Villareal knew how to make an entrance.

As Random had been told, Villareal was tall for a native. He looked like a figure out of legend on his great horse, with his black frock coat and the dreaded White Hood that always covered his face. The coat was open, and Random raised the binoculars for a closer look.

Gonzalez and Bacon had both spoken of the distinctive matched pistols Villareal carried. It was too far to identify the revolver thrust through *El Jefe*'s belt as a Walker Colt in this light, but it was definitely a huge weapon not unlike the Walker. But they had insisted there was a pair of the Colts, and here was only one.

There was no time to ponder the question. Pistols got lost easily, especially on desperate midnight rides over rough terrain. For that matter, at this range the binoculars did not pick up the silver crucifix Villareal was said to wear. But he might have kept it inside his shirt.

The man on the high horse waved, and his four retainers—the guards Pacheco had mentioned—faded into the darkness. The great man was sending out sentries himself. Random was grimly amused.

For once the *gorras'* leader had made an error. Or, rather, he was making the proper move too late. The wolf was already among the fold. All Villareal had accomplished was to make the wolf's job easier.

The chief of the night riders dismounted and strode to a humpbacked boulder, his coat trailing majestically behind him. He climbed up to stand atop the boulder. When he spoke his voice was distorted by the hood he wore. Random realized why no one had definitely identified this man as Noe Villareal— not only did he keep his features hidden, his true voice was masked as effectively as his face by the cloth *gorra*. His voice was strong, though with distance and the rumbling mutter of men and horses Random could not make out the words, despite the fact that he was picking Spanish up rapidly.

He drew his rifle up beside him. Working by touch he grasped the bolt and slid a stubby cartridge into place in the chamber with a scarcely audible click. For insurance, he told himself.

But that wasn't all, and he knew it. That rifle had a sliding sight that would adjust to a thousand meters. How far away was *El Jefe*'s broad, vulnerable chest? A hundred, perhaps. The weapon was of Swiss manufacture, an 1878 .41 caliber Vetterli, and like the sawed-off shotgun in his coat pocket was a specialized tool of his trade. Random was not alone in considering it the finest military long arm of the day. It was a temptation to make use of its awesome striking power. A slight pressure on the trigger and *El Jefe*'s ringing voice would be stilled forever.

He put the thought from him. It was foolishness. He knew very well he couldn't take the easy way and shoot the *gorra* in cold blood. He'd made his plans and would stick to them.

In fact, things were looking simpler than he'd expected. Villareal had a passion for secrecy as well as a dramatic streak. Random conjectured he would slip away once he'd finished speaking, giving no one a chance to follow him—perhaps trusted lieutenants would keep the mob in the clearing so nobody could try to pierce *El Jefe*'s cloak of mystery. There would be a time before Villareal rejoined his bodyguards—if he did. It might amuse him to disappear completely when his speech was over like some spirit of night and revolution. Either way Random thought he saw the perfect opportunity to take his quarry unawares and alone.

He never knew afterward what alerted him that something untoward was happening. He was just slithering backward out of his stone shooting blind when *El Jefe*'s voice rose to a crescendo. Random caught the word *"gringo"* and looked back into the hollow.

Men were up and running, drawing their pistols, leaping into the saddles of horses. *El Jefe* was gesticulating furiously. And a knot of angry White Hoods were running up the grassy slope of the bowl, right at Random's hiding place.

Impossibly, Noe Villareal had been warned.

Random moved fast. If Pacheco knew of the rock-jumble hiding place it was a good bet other *gorras* did too. Or perhaps the wall-eyed *nativo* had sold Random out. It didn't matter either way; it was time to go before the old saw about hunted turning on the hunter came true.

He straightened. To the right he saw a bobbing whiteness. It was a man's head covered by a hood. The *gorra* rounded the rocks and stopped dead, six feet away.

Reflex took over. The native's warning cry came out a voiceless whoosh of expelled air as the butt of the Vetterli slammed into his stomach. He doubled over with a choking, gagging retch, and Random raised his rifle for the killing stroke to the back of the neck, trademark of the Legionnaire.

He checked himself barely in time. *No unnecessary killing, remember?* he chided himself. Instead of breaking the man's neck he slugged him in the head hard enough to put him out for the night.

An idea came to Random. One man in a mask looks much like another. He stooped and tore off the hood. . . .

. . . And found himself looking into the unconscious features of Roberto Morales.

Just my luck, he thought. But he felt a certain relief. Elena's fears for the boy had turned out to be justified—Roberto had just been brushed by the man on the black camel, but now he was out of danger.

Horses crashed through the brush on both sides as Random ran stooped over for the stand of trees where his mare was tethered. There was no time for fancy dodging. A *gorra* ranging ahead of the baying pack might stumble across the horse at any moment.

Though he had Roberto's hood for a disguise, he didn't dare put it on yet. He couldn't stop and he couldn't risk running full tilt into a tree while pulling it on and trying to find the eyeholes. He could only keep his head down and run.

Tree limbs crackled close by. Random was in the open, between sheltering clumps of pine. He stopped and whirled, the Vetterli in firing position at his hip.

For one endless instant they were frozen, the crouching youth in the blue coat and the hooded horseman. The Vetterli was aimed at the raider's midsection, but the *gorra* had a cocked pistol leveled at Random. Then the rider lowered the gun. He gestured urgently.

Random recognized the horse. *Pacheco!*

Random's finger stayed curled around the trigger. Had the renegade *gorra* turned his coat again and sold him out? His only chance at survival lay in trusting the native.

The Vetterli dipped toward the ground. Pacheco reared the sorrel and turned its head. He spurred into the woods at a breakneck gallop. A moment later Random heard him yelling—"This way! *Amigos*, I've found him!" A great commotion followed his voice, away from Random. He was leading the enraged *gorras* on a wild-goose chase.

With relief Random pulled Roberto's mask on. He was now one White Hood among many. His mare was scratching her rag-wrapped nose on the bole of a tree when he sprinted up, lungs burning, old wound throbbing. Scarlet pain pulsed behind his eyes. Shots and cries rang confusedly at his back as he freed the horse, sprang into the saddle, and rode hell-bent for home.

For many ragged breaths he listened for the hammering hoofbeats of pursuit. But the outcry dwindled to nothing and the only sound was the steady drumming of the gray's feet.

He'd failed in his attempt to capture his foe. But a fierce exultation flowed in his veins like fire.

The *gorras* would long remember this night. So would Random. He had been sold out to the raiders.

And someone would pay.

CHAPTER ELEVEN

It was after midnight when Random rode his lathered mare up to the San Rael schoolhouse. "Mr. Gorman," Dave Sherman yelled from the front steps, "it's Mr. Random—he's back!"

The ex-sergeant charged out the door, fully dressed, as Random had known he'd be. "Thank God you're back," Gorman cried. "Two of the lookouts came in twenty minutes ago, saying they'd heard gunfire to the north. We were just about to come after you, orders or not. What the hell happened?"

Random dismounted and grimly told the story. "But what's wrong?" Gorman demanded when he'd finished. "You lit a fire under them! They know they ain't safe any more, even on their own hunting grounds."

"But how did they *know*? Someone told Villareal I'd be somewhere nearby. It wasn't Pa—my informant. He's the one who drew them off my trail."

Gorman shrugged his sturdy shoulders. "Could've been a wild hunch. Villareal must know you're gunning for him, and this is the first time he's shown himself since you been here."

Random shook his head disgustedly. "He won't show himself again. But I still have to catch him. *Merde*." He gave a weary sigh. "I need to ride to Los Duranes tomorrow to look into this challenge the *nativos* are so scared of. I will send a telegram to a man I know, who may be able to dig up some more detailed information about Villareal. I have to know more before I can try to draw him out."

He rose with the sun and rode for the largest town in Duran County. Before visiting the courthouse, Random went to the Western Union office on Broad Street, by the hotel. He already knew what he wanted to say, so he drew out a yellow telegram blank.

The one real clue he had to Villareal's activities between leaving his hometown and returning to it was the robbery-murder in Durango. If the town marshal was looking for Villareal, he might well know more about him than Random had been able to find out so far.

The telegram he wrote out was not addressed to the Durango marshal, however. Random was, after all, only a private citizen. The marshal could hardly be expected to take the time to dig up background information on a fugitive for anyone who happened to have the price of a telegram. Instead Random was sending the wire to one of his few friends in the land of his birth, a one-eyed ex-major named Kelly. It had been Garth Kelly who pulled strings to help straighten out the delicate matter of Random's citizenship when he tried to re-enter the United States. He had left illegally and complicated matters by serving in the armed forces of another country, which is forbidden to American citizens by the Constitution. Kelly had aided him then, and Random hoped he would now as well.

For Garth Kelly was now a top administrator with the Pinkertons. And while local lawmen often felt little love for the "eye that never sleeps," the Durango marshal would be more likely to cooperate with Kelly than to refuse.

Random wrote:

URGENT PLEASE QUERY MARSHAL DURANGO COLORADO INFORMATION REGARDING NOE VILLAREAL

WANTED BANK ROBBERY AND MURDER SUMMER 1882
STOP RANDOM END

Finishing, he walked to the window and pushed
the sheet at a bored-looking clerk with a green eye-
shade. The clerk glanced over the page while Random leaned on the counter. He asked a couple of
questions, then figured the cost. Random paid him.

"It will take a day or two for the reply to come
back," Random told the clerk. "I cannot wait here
for it, but I need the answer as soon as possible.
Could you arrange to have it delivered to me in San
Rael?"

The clerk gazed at him with frank disbelief.

Random raised his hand from the counter. A shiny
yellow coin lay there. The clerk's eyes grew wider as
they took in the eagle embossed on it.

"Of course, I'd expect to pay for the service," Random said dryly. "And it would be only reasonable for
you to receive a compensation for your trouble as
well."

The clerk nodded. The twenty-dollar gold piece
went to wherever twenty-dollar gold pieces go.
"Thank you very much, sir," the clerk said with lots
of oil. It was probably as much money as he made in
a month. "I'll see to it that it is delivered promptly,
sir."

Random touched his hat and went out smiling.

At the courthouse Random was informed that he
had missed the county clerk by a few minutes. Mr.
Rule would be back at one, a hefty matron lady told
him. With an hour and a half to kill, Random ate a
steak, home fries, and coffee at the hotel, then drifted
into the gun shop.

The gunsmith greeted Random in a friendly fashion. With time on his hands, Random fell into conversation with the man. In a short while he went out
and came back with the long rifle that rode in a boot
beneath his left stirrup.

"This is the Vetterli, Model 1878," Random said, handing it across the counter. The skinny little smith, a yellow-eyed man with an old-young face, accepted the weapon almost reverentially.

"I've heard a great deal about this piece," he said, "but I never expected to lay eyes on one. You know the history of it?"

Random nodded. "The Swiss were getting edgy with both Bismarck and Louis Napoleon crowding their frontiers. They wanted something better than the Chassepots and needle-guns their neighbors had."

"So they came up with this beauty," the gunsmith said, turning the Vetterli over in his hands.

"In 1865. It's rimfire, doesn't have the overlong firing pin of the Dreyse nor the fragile rubber stopper of the Chassepot. It carries ten rounds in a tubular magazine, more than either of the other bolt-actions, and is one hell of a lot more accurate." He smiled and rubbed his chin. "Neither the French nor the Prussians were too eager to try their luck against angry Swiss armed with the things in those high mountain passes."

"It's only .41 caliber, though. We have repeaters too, like the Winchester. Good, lever-action .44s."

Random snorted. "With all due respect, m'sieur, the Winchester fires a pistol round, for God's sake. Past a hundred and fifty yards or so, you might as well throw rocks." He took the weapon back from the wizened smith. "Besides, while a lever action is faster, it's much more difficult to keep under cover when you're firing one. You have to turn the piece sideways, or chance hunching yourself accidentally into the other fellow's field of fire. With a bolt action, you just slide it back and forth, without going through any silly contortions."

He glanced at his watch. He had a few minutes yet before the Duran county clerk returned from eating lunch. "Have you ever seen a Walker Colt?" he asked.

The gunsmith bobbed his head. "Once or twice.

They're a mite rare, son. Mostly belong to Texas Rangers, and they don't cotton to parting with their pieces."

"Have you ever heard of a native owning one? Or, say, a pair of Walkers?"

It was the older man's turn to snort. "A Mexican?" He laughed. "Son, you must be pulling my leg. A Ranger would hardly be likely to *sell* his gun to a Mex, now would he?" He shook his head. "No, to have a Walker, not to mention having a pair of 'em, a Mex would have to be a mighty hard case. He'd just about have to take them off a dead Ranger, and that ain't an easy task. That Walker is quite a gun, my boy. A lot more than, say, that Peacemaker you've got."

Random nodded. The information he had indicated that Noe Villareal was a fairly tough customer—a "hard case," as the gunsmith had said. This only confirmed what he knew already.

He checked his watch again. It was five minutes of one. He bought a box of ammunition for his Colt and walked out to keep his appointment with the county clerk.

According to Mrs. Vardeman, the population of the two San Raels was just about a thousand. Los Duranes, the county seat, twenty miles to the north, had half again as many people. A coal mine had brought both the larger population and larger importance.

When Random had ridden in under leaden skies that morning, Los Duranes had been alive with activity. People thronged the boardwalks, many wearing Eastern-style clothing rather than the more rugged Western dress of San Rael. The prosperous county seat of an otherwise poor county had all the amenities of modern life: banks, a hotel, the telegraph office, a saloon with a thirty-foot hardwood bar that was the pride of the Territory. It also possessed the county courthouse, though, oddly, not the sheriff—for some reason his headquarters were back in San Rael—and that was where Random headed now.

The courthouse clock was just chiming one o'clock when Random walked through the door. Overhead the clouds were getting thicker. A storm was on the way, and he hoped it would hold off until he got back to San Rael.

Mr. Rule, the county clerk, was back from his meal. He was a lean, long-jawed, balding man, but surprisingly affable despite the fact that he looked for all the world like an undertaker. "Lawsuit?" he asked, shaking Random's hand with his spidery fingers. "So you want to know about the San Rael lawsuit."

So there is a suit, after all, Random thought as the clerk ushered him into the tiny, musty cubicle that served as Rule's office. It was wood paneled and full of ancient dust. Rule sat behind his desk, motioning Random to take the other chair. He pulled a book from a shelf behind him. He blew a cloud of dust from it and consulted the book while Random had a coughing fit.

"Ah," the clerk said with evident satisfaction. He popped a red and white striped peppermint into his mouth to ease his digestion and put the book back. Folding his thin pale hands on the blotter, he peered at Random with disconcertingly black eyes.

"The suit that has been filed concerning land ownership in the San Rael area has as its object a re-determination of the boundaries of certain land belonging, I understand, to a number of the native citizens." Random nodded.

"Allow me to explain a few points of land law, then," Rule said. "In most cases, the land owned by natives here in the Territory is grant land, ceded to them by the Spanish monarchy centuries ago. Now, the description of the lands in question was invariably more poetic than scientific. For example, the land granted to a Señor Such-and-such might extend, say, 'from the lightning-struck tree to the *ciénega*'—

that's a hog's-back ridge, Mr. Random—'and in breadth will extend from the sweet water spring as far as a man may ride between sunup and sundown.' As you may have guessed, I am quoting an actual grant."

The clerk pursed his thin lips and shook his head. "Now, at best, the exact boundaries set by such a grant, which is referred to as a metes-and-bounds deed, are open to argument. Even when the actual area was alluded to it was imprecise, since units of area tended to change from viceroy to viceroy."

He finished off his mint with a crunch of his long horsy teeth. "When such metes-and-bounds deeds are challenged in court, the holders of the land under litigation often find their holdings diminish considerably. In particular, when the landowners have brown skins and the challengers are of a markedly lighter hue, if you get my drift, sir. As a matter of fact, such depredations against native-owned land were rampant, to the point of causing a scandal that brought down the last Territorial administration. You may have heard of the Santa Fe Ring?"

"Yes."

"They had, shall we say, a great deal of influence with judges in the Territory. They encountered little difficulty in having metes-and-bounds redetermined to suit their desires." The clerk squinted at his visitor. With the clouds gathering, the sunlight that filtered in through the fly-specked window was weak. "Given this information, I imagine you would say that the natives in San Rael will be rather inconvenienced by the suit?" he asked.

"I would say so, yes." Inside Random was seething with rage at the shortsighted dolt who had brought the suit. He could scarcely conceive of such idiocy.

Rule sat back with a knowing smile. "You would be quite wrong," he said. "When the suit comes to a hearing next month, the judge will promptly throw it out of court."

Random gaped at him, causing his smile to widen.

"You see, young man, the land belonging to the natives of San Rael is not delineated by metes and bounds, but by survey. And while even surveyed land boundaries can be challenged, the court—the present court, things having changed somewhat since the heyday of the Santa Fe Ring—will not uphold any such challenge."

"I don't understand," the younger man confessed.

"It seems that in 1855 the natives had some manner of legal adviser. That was the year of the coal strike here in Duran County. To protect themselves, the natives themselves bought suit to have the boundaries of the land redetermined."

When Random responded to this with a look of total confusion, Rule explained. "Because the suit had been brought, the land was surveyed. Perhaps because no mineral deposits were found on or near the native-owned property, the proceedings simply amounted to having the court recognize officially the rights of the natives to the land they claimed. All quite legal and, in practice, almost ironclad."

Random whistled appreciatively. "Could I see the filing papers?" he asked.

"Of course. They are public record." Rule unfolded his scarecrow body from his swivel chair and walked out of the office. Random sat still, turning over what he'd just learned.

In a few moments Rule returned. He placed a manila folder on the desk in front of Random. The young man picked it up and leafed through the papers. The legal terms were gibberish to Random; what he was looking for was a signature.

"Raymond N. Mason?"

"The man who filed the suit," Rule stated.

"Who is he?"

"I have no idea."

Random tossed the folder back onto the desk. A cloud of dust billowed up where it landed. "Why was the suit filed?" he asked. "Wasn't this Mason advised it was useless?"

"Of course he was," the clerk said. "As to why he went ahead with it, I can only venture a guess—a very unofficial one, mind you."

"I'd be obliged."

"It strikes me that the natives probably no longer have such a wise counselor as they had in 1855, if they have any at all," Rule said deliberately. "Consequently, the simple filing of the suit would frighten them, since they would have no way of knowing it had no chance of success. The man filing the suit—or the people he represents—could conceivably offer the natives a ludicrously low sum of money for their property, on the grounds that it is preferable to sell and realize some profit than have the land taken away outright."

Stunned, Random sat stroking his chin. It was beginning to seem that the suit was a stroke of genius rather than idiocy. But only if the man whose idea it was also had some way of dealing with the Anglos who did not want to part with their land. They stood in the way of the proposed railroad as well as the *nativos.*

The gorras! Random thought. He frowned. Could they be a tool, somehow, to do the work of intimidating the whites while the bugaboo of the challenge was scaring the Mexicans? Was Villareal unwittingly helping some unknown party rob his people of their homes? Or was he a knowing party?

The implications were staggering. Cal Sharper, knowing that Random had contacts with the *nativos* —*El Jefe* knowing that Random would be present last night—a sinister answer to these mysteries began to suggest itself to Random.

Something was going on in San Rael, of which Random had had no inkling up until this very moment. And his life could depend on his getting to the bottom of it very, very soon.

CHAPTER TWELVE

The countryside spread out in a vast panorama of muted colors beneath the gray, low-hanging clouds. Here and there in the distance the sun broke through, tinting the mountains yellow. Rain smell hung in the air. Random raced the coming storm to San Rael.

He kept his plucky little mare to a steady, ground-eating trot. The flies were twice as active as usual. The horse was plagued especially by deerflies, insects the size and shape of houseflies, but with opaque wings like a moths, patterned tan and brown. Random killed a dozen of them, and several of the bigger, nastier horseflies.

The road from Los Duranes to San Rael curved westward around the snowcapped Hermanas, then wound like a serpent about a number of lesser mountains. Random passed the Sisters, feeling the wind freshen, feeling the bite of rain almost ready to fall. He hoped the storm wouldn't catch him on the exposed slope.

He heard the sharp *crack!* of the first bullet's passage well before he heard the sound of the shot. Ahead, a puff of white smoke was whipped by the wind away from the mountainside.

Without waiting for the smoke blossom of a second shot Random dove off the mare, dragging the snorting beast off the causeway by main force. Loose pebbles slid under hooves and boots. The gray slipped, fell on her side with a grunt.

Random yanked the Vetterli from its scabbard, which was luckly on the side the mare hadn't fallen onto. A bullet hit a rock nearby and whined off into space. The mare regained her feet and clambered back onto the road, then set off for San Rael at a lope. Random threw himself face down in a clump of stunted *piñon*. Another shot rang out up the mountain. He never heard the ball go past.

Behind his boot soles, Random could hear the gravel rattling down the slope and over the lip of a sheer cliff. He had cut it awfully close. Another two feet and he and the gray would have gone over to their deaths.

Random scanned the mountainside for his ambushers. Obligingly, a flurry of gunfire broke out from the scree-littered slope. Several shots went by with a sound like the snapping of a whip, much too high. Two slugs kicked dirt at the edge of the road.

From the smoke, Random counted three gunmen, spread out across thirty yards, just below where tall trees crowned the slope. He flipped his sight to two hundred meters. It was a poor ambush, though his enemies, whoever they were, had found themselves a good spot. The riflemen were too close together and had only one angle of fire. In the mountains of North Africa a trio of ambushers would have arranged themselves with two men well apart upslope and one down between the roadway and the precipice. The victim would be permitted to pass the first man on the mountainside before all three opened up in a three-way crossfire from which it would be next to impossible to find cover. And even if the first volley missed the man, it would have killed his horse. A man on foot is easier game. As it was, Random would only have to walk a half mile or so to recover his mount, which he knew he would find placidly cropping the rabbit grass that grew beside the causeway.

Of course, to retrieve the mare, Random would have to survive his present predicament. He was still outnumbered three to one. But he had teeth, as the unidentified bushwhackers were about to discover.

Movement flickered in his field of vision, a patch of paleness among the rocks. Patiently he held his fire. Two more shots came his way. Random saw the moving white thing jerk, and then smoke billowed from the same spot.

Random smiled grimly and spat out a mouthful of dust. As he'd told the gunsmith in Los Duranes, a man with a lever action had an unfortunate tendency to expose himself from low cover. And that was just what was happening up among the rocks. The bobbing patch of white was somebody's head—covered by a white cloth hood.

He felt honored in a way. As far as Random knew, this was the first daylight appearance of the *gorras.* Before this they had only donned their white masks when they had had the additional protection of darkness.

Random laid the sights of his rifle on the gunman's partially exposed head. The *gorra* was sitting or kneeling behind his rock, undoubtedly convinced he was completely hidden from his quarry's view. His two companions, however, offered Random no target whatsoever. All he could see of them was their gunsmoke when they fired.

The light was poor, the wind bad and getting worse. Uphill shots were always a tricky proposition. And if Random fired and missed he would spook the incautious raider into covering himself better. If that happened, Random's outlook would be bleak. Even ambushers as inept as these would soon realize they weren't going to get their man this way. Then it would be simple for two of them to make Random keep his head down by firing as fast as they could pump in the cartridges, while the third man slipped down and flanked the youth.

If Random backed up a few feet he'd be standing on nothing but two hundred feet of air, and if he tried to run, the *gorras* would blast him over the edge. Once the ambushers wised up and tried the flanking maneuver, he was dead. As the situation stood, though, his Vetterli gave him an edge in accuracy over his enemies' stubby Winchesters.

The White Hoods were getting impatient. They started to lay down a hail of lead. In the center, the man Random could see began firing like clockwork. After every shot, his head shifted up slightly as he levered the next round into the chamber. If he did not know that in this business you avoided predictable regularity like the plague, that was his lookout. Random timed him, drawing a deep breath.

Bang!—bang!—bang! barked the repeater.

When the third cloud of smoke appeared Random pulled the trigger. The heavy Vetterli roared and slammed into his shoulder.

Six hundred feet away the crouching rifleman feverishly worked the lever of his carbine. As always, the motion hunched his head a fraction of an inch upward as he brought the cartridge home.

At fifteen hundred feet a second, the .41 ball hit him just above the right eye.

Random saw fragments of skull and torn cloth fly. The *gorra* came halfway erect before falling back. Even from that distance Random could see that he was dead.

The other two rifles fell silent. The click of Random working his bolt sounded like a shot in the sudden stillness.

Random let go a ragged sigh. He had taken a desperate flyer and knew it. He was a fine marksman, but that shot had been almost pure luck. He wasn't about to complain about it.

The survivors of the ambush party looked at each other. Their opening arguments had left their opponent untouched, whereas his first reply had scored a telling point. With that, they lost their taste for further debate.

A raider slithered from cover on his belly, clutching his carbine. Random saw him and took aim, but held his fire. He allowed the *gorra* to reach the dead man's side. When the first man made it alive, his companion crawled over. The Vetterli's muzzle swung to cover him, but the rifle remained silent.

In a moment the two *nativos* sprang up like a brace of flushed quail. They had their fallen comrade between them. His boots dragged the ground as they hauled him up the slope. Random threw several fast shots into the dirt at their heels before they reached the cover of the trees, to let them know he was still there. Then they were gone.

The stars were out of sight above the low-slung clouds when Random rode up to the Gonzalez house. Inside Gonzalez and his daughter were most likely sitting down to a late dinner, after the native fashion. Random hated to disturb their meal, but he had urgent business with Gonzalez.

Reining in, Random leapt to the ground. As he made for the door a figure detached itself from the shadows at the corner of the house. Random froze at the glint of steel in the yellow light from the windows.

It was Joselito, the mute Indian. The Pueblo gazed at him impassively, then lowered his cocked carbine. *"Buenas noches,"* Random told him. He turned toward the door.

Joselito slipped by him and ushered him into the *sala.* In the dining room the portly rancher and his daughter had just stood up from the table. "Señor Random," Gonzalez nodded. He saw the rifle in his servant's hand. "I apologize. Since the gathering of the *viejos* we are . . . wary."

Random's mouth quirked. It was wise of Gonzalez to take precautions. Particularly when the *gorras* were scared enough to try to ambush the Anglos' mercenary in broad daylight.

Elena looked alarmed. "Your clothes!" she exclaimed. "Are you—?"

"I'm undamaged," Random said, dropping his hat onto the white *banco*. "I was—how do you say?—dry-gulched by three of our friends with the hoods. I killed one and let the others run off. I lay up under cover until nightfall, in case they were hanging around out of sight."

The girl's face was unreadable. Random knew Elena was torn by her relief at his escape and her fear for Roberto's safety. As it was, the youth reminded himself, she had not yet heard of Roberto's close call the night before. The *nativa* despised the *gorras*, but Random doubted that affected her feelings for young Morales much.

She had no doubt convinced herself Roberto was only a sympathizer, not an active member. Random did not feel obliged to disillusion her.

As concisely as he could, Random told Gonzalez what he had learned in Los Duranes. "I do not understand what is happening," he confessed when he had finished. "But I'm certain there is more going on in San Rael than anyone suspects."

"A plot, señor?"

"If you will."

Gonzalez shook his head firmly. "Then this *El Jefe* cannot be Noe Villareal. He would not be part of any plot that would hurt his own people. Not deliberately, *amigo*. And he would certainly see through it if any Anglos were using the *gorras* for their own ends. If that is what is happening."

"It's too much of a coincidence," Random said. "The ploy of having this Mason file a phony suit is apparently part of a larger plan. Look at it—the *gorras* terrorize the Anglos into wanting to sell, while Mason's backers wave the suit under the noses of your *nativos.* Are you sure you have never heard of Raymond Mason?"

"No," Gonzalez said. "It does sound almost familiar, but I cannot place the name." He paused. "You must see now, my young Anglo friend, Noe Villareal has no part in these raids."

"I know you respect the man, and your sense of justice can't bear to see him wrongly accused," Random said, "but the evidence still points right to him. Another coincidence: He's run out of town and goes into hiding and *voilà!* The *gorras blancas* are founded by a tall *nativo* with a big pistol like the one Villareal carries, who hides by day and never lets his face be seen."

"*Sí*, no one has seen *El Jefe*'s face. And the man only carries one pistol. Where is the other? Noe was proud of his matched pair of fine weapons. And where is the crucifix his dying father gave to him?"

"He probably keeps it hidden. It's distinctive."

"So is that ancient *pistola,* señor."

Random sighed. "Then he could have lost the crucifix. I don't like that detail either. But the facts still point to Villareal being *El Jefe.*" The round native still looked unconvinced. Random felt enormously tired. "The important thing now is to get to Mr. Mason and have some answers."

"I hope you find him quickly. The lawsuit will not be heard till next month. The *viejos* will not accept your assurances that the challenge will be dismissed. They trust you, my friend, but they have no reason to trust an Anglo court."

Random's next destination was the Barnes's mansion. Lacey peered timidly around the edge of the door in answer to his knock, then let him in. The sky was sprinkling rain, but the clouds had not yet opened the way they'd been threatening to all day.

Late as it was, Junella was up pacing the floor of the parlor. "Oh, Mr. Random, I'm so glad to see you," she said as he came in. "I'm worried about

Uncle—*Mister Random!* What's *happened* to you?"

Random told her about the ambush on the Los Duranes road. "Those filthy, murdering black Mexican devils," the girl said furiously, making Random wince.

"I've got to speak with your uncle," he told her.

"I'm afraid you can't," she said, shaking her head. "He had an attack this afternoon. Terrible pains in his back. He can hardly stir out of bed. Doctor says he thinks it's the change in the weather."

As she spoke Random became aware of the warm bundle of femininity not an arm's length from him. He put his hands on her shoulders. She put her head to one side, half-shutting her big blue eyes.

Random shook himself. There were more than enough complications in his young life at the moment without adding Clay Barnes's lovely ward to the list. Maybe later, when the job was done.

That time was looking steadily more remote. Damn Mason, whoever he was, and this halfwit lawsuit. Or the careful conspiracy, whichever it was. One thing Random knew. Once he got his hands on Raymond N. Mason the man would do some rapid talking.

Exhaustion was pulling at his shoulders. Night after night of chasing raiders, and his unsuccessful nocturnal stalking of *El Jefe* had left him little time for sleep. Without another word he leaned forward and kissed the blonde girl on the forehead. Then he left.

At the schoolhouse his men were asleep in their bedrolls, snoring like a chorus of crosscut saws. Russ Gorman was out sitting on an arroyo bank north of town, waiting for the hooded night riders to come. This did not look like Random's night to find out who the mysterious and troublesome Mr. Mason was.

Well, Mason would presumably be the same tomorrow. Random unrolled his blankets on a vacant stretch of floor and was sound asleep in an instant.

It seemed he had no more than lowered his weary head onto his rolled coat when shouts awakened him.

Shouts and shots. He staggered to his feet, knowing that something was hideously, irretrievably wrong. He jumped over the groggily stirring forms on the floor and ran out the door.

The dull red glow underlighting the clouds above the ridgeline confirmed his sudden sick suspicion.

The night riders had struck across the wide-open, cowhand filled meadow. Had struck the safe, southern side of town.

CHAPTER THIRTEEN

By the time Random and his men reached the burning farmhouse, the heavens had at last burst open and spilled a torrent of rain on the troubled hills. The rain quenched the flames before the *vigas*, the thick beams supporting the house's roof, could burn through. The roof went, but the damage that the fire did could easily be repaired. Wet and frightened, the residents of the stricken house were wrapped in blankets and dispersed to neighbors' homes for the night.

The man of the house was not home when the raiders hit. He was watching the eastern arroyo trail while the *gorras* circled west and south. His name was Bob Chase, and he was one of Random's volunteer riders.

Another coincidence? the youthful mercenary asked himself as the flames hissed and died in the sheeting rain.

He didn't think so.

There was nothing to be done at the Chase location. The owner came back as soon as a hard-riding messenger could fetch him. Random steeled himself, waiting for the man's accusations.

They never came. Chase merely looked at the young man sadly. "You done what you could, friend," he said. "Nobody would have figgered the Mexes'd come up across the high pastures. How the hell did they get past them cowboys up there, anyways?"

It was another question Random would have liked to have an answer for. He didn't see any way to get

one now, however. The raiders were long gone, their
tracks wiped away by the rain, and so he went back to
the schoolhouse and got what sleep time and his
thoughts allowed.

The storm let up at daybreak. Random rose with
the gray and washed-out dawn. He saddled the mare
and rode out across the meadow. He had no chance
of finding any sign of where the raiders had gone, nor
how they had crossed under the eye of the cowhands
stationed on the range.

All he wanted was the chance to be alone, to think.
The successful night attack had damaged his prestige
and strengthened the resolve of the wavering *gorras*.
It would without question increase hostility toward
the Mexicans among Random's employers—and sympathy for Tag Carroll's ideas about solving the problem of the raids. And all this before the youth had
time to digest the stunning news he'd gotten at the
county seat.

It seemed the whole world was conniving at his
downfall.

While Random was on his solitary ride, disaster hit.

A rancher coming into town for some feed, flour,
and a new axehead at McMurphey's Mercantile
passed Cal Sharper, Jerry Moody, and two of Sharper's other young sidekicks, headed for the Mexican
village. They looked to have taken on a skinful at
Turk's, as the rancher put it when he told one of the
men at the schoolhouse. The boys were laughing and
in general seemed pretty full of themselves.

Expecting trouble, Webb Gordon rode out after
Sharper with Bruce MacCaleb and Mike Hunt, two
more members of Random's patrol, while Dave Sherman set out in search of the absent mercenary.

The trio missed Sharper and company, only to be
met at the outskirts of the *nativo* settlement with a
fusillade of rifle fire that left MacCaleb and Gordon
bleeding from flesh wounds. Pulling back, they looked

for and found a native who in better times had been a friend of MacCaleb's.

The man was middle-aged and gaunt, no *gorra*, and he shook with fear lest someone see him in the company of *gringos* as he told his story. Before long the three Anglos knew why he was so afraid.

Sharper and his partners had ridden through the village at a gallop, firing their six-shooters into the air with drunken abandon. Even in an area where Mexican and Anglo lived together in peace as they had in San Rael before the present troubles, the *nativos* had learned that in a case like this the only thing to do was keep their heads down and curse the sodden gunslingers.

But one door had been flung open as the riders passed. Sharper had caught the movement from the corner of his eye, and his lightning reflexes put a shot through the doorway before his whiskey-addled brain realized what was happening.

The bullet had hit a four-year-old girl, killing her instantly. Not having learned the caution of her elders, she had wanted to see what was going on outside. It sounded so exciting.

Suddenly very, very sober, the four Anglo youngsters had fled the village, heading right out overland for their own town.

Even as Gordon told the story back at the schoolhouse, a boy came running to say Sharper was back at Turk's with his friends. With still more whiskey under their belts, they were bragging about what had happened, or rather Sharper was bragging. The others were acting subdued and scared. Sheriff Hoopwright had barricaded himself in his office and was not budging.

"Bragging?" Gordon said disgustedly. "What the hell was he saying?"

"He—he said he was glad he'd killed the little greaser bitch, sir," the boy stammered. " 'Nits make lice,' he said, Cal did."

Gorman went white under his tan. "Nits make lice" had been a favorite saying of Colonel John Chivington, of the Colorado Third Volunteer Cavalry. For a moment Gorman was a raw recruit riding toward the Indian camp at Sand Creek, Colorado. He saw again the circling birds, smelled the stench of the untended dead. *God, the crumpled bodies!* The words brought them back before his eyes. He saw them, women, men, ancients of either sex—and the children. So many. He had been unable to eat for a week. And he still had the dreams.

"Little snake's talkin' big," MacCaleb opined. He was still holding a red-soaked handkerchief to his arm where a native bullet had winged him. "Figgers Carroll will get some boys together to protect him, before Random gets back."

"Sent Dave after Random," Gorman said mechanically.

"Carroll'll have Cal hidden out somewheres safe afore Dave finds him, I reckon," Mike Hunt said.

Without a word, Ross Gorman picked his old Springfield up by the barrel and walked toward the door of the schoolroom. "Where the hell you goin'?" Gordon called after him.

"Down to Turk's."

"You cain't go by your lonesome, dammit. That Sharper kid's crazy as a rabid wolf pup. He'll gun you, sure."

"I'm bringing him in," Gorman said. "And you're staying here."

No one followed him out. The men all recognized this was something special between Gorman and the murderous youth. Besides, what if they did go along? There was apt to be a full-scale gun battle. And nobody had much stomach for having to shoot down fellow whites.

The street was a gluey mass of mud. The sky hung low. A thin drizzle was falling, and people walked with hats pulled low and collars pulled high. A man walking toward the *cantina* saw Gorman and changed his mind about stopping in for a quick shot. From the look on the ex-scout's face, it didn't look as if Turk's was going to be a very healthy vicinity before long.

A heavy oaken door was closed against the weather, over the swinging doors. Gorman pulled it open and pushed through the double doors.

The room was lit by kerosene lanterns. Sharper was propped on the bar in the midst of his cronies, frozen in the act of putting a half-full whiskey bottle to his lips. A pale blue eye rolled at Gorman and went slitted.

Instinctively, Sharper's friends edged back. "Put the bottle down, Cal," Gorman said, speaking in that formal tone men of that day often used when blood was about to spill. "You are coming with me now."

Slowly Sharper lowered the bottle, his gaze icy, pinned to Gorman. A lock of crow's-wing hair fell over one eye. "Back off, Russ," he said with false heartiness. "You ain't a deputy like your pal Random. Don't go borrowin' trouble."

"Don't hand me that shit, Sharper," Gorman said. The muzzle of the trap door swung up to aim dead center of the youth's fancy belt buckle of Mexican silver. "Put that bottle down and come along. Or be carried out. I don't care which way, and that's a fact."

Sharper shrugged. "Hey, partner, no trouble," he said easily, smiling.

Then he threw the bottle right at Gorman's face.

The ball from Gorman's army rifle splintered the bar where Sharper had stood a second before. Sharper hit the floor with his gun out. He fired six times as the former sergeant of scouts turned toward him.

Blood starting from holes in his chest, Gorman staggered back into the wall, upsetting tables and chairs. The Springfield dropped from his hand. He stood there glaring hate at Sharper while men scrambled to get out of the way.

On the sawdust-covered floor Sharper waited for the mortally wounded man to fall. But he didn't. Gorman fumbled inside his shirt while blood streamed over his hands.

He brought out a broad-bladed skinning knife. Teeth clenched, face drained of blood, he forced himself away from the wall. Blood smeared the plaster where he'd stood.

Frantically Sharper clawed out his other pistol. "Go down, damn you! *Go down!*" he howled. He fired twice. Gorman was slammed back into the wall. He blinked twice as if puzzled by something. A froth of blood touched his lips. His every muscle straining, his square face twisted with agony and superhuman effort, Russ Gorman started for his opponent one more time.

"Die, damn you! *Die!*" Sharper screamed, his voice cracking with terror. His next shot blew off the side of Gorman's head. Gorman collapsed like a rag doll. His boot heels kicked once at the floorboards, and then he was still.

A crowd had gathered before the schoolhouse. Dave Sherman and Random dismounted on its fringes and made their way through to the front steps. Men fell back to let them pass.

Russ Gorman lay on a blood-dyed blanket spread out on the teacher's desk. Dr. Stern straightened from his side, shaking his head.

Without speaking, Random turned on his heel and walked out.

The oaken door at Turk's opened. The smaller inner doors banged into the walls as Random pushed through. His right hand was out of sight inside his long *capote*. The skin was stretched over his cheekbones seemingly taut enough to burst, and the red brand burned out of his fury-whitened face.

Heads turned. Again men backed away from the

line of fire. Turk threw up his hands and went into the back room, shaking his head in disgust.

There would shortly be more blood to clean off his floors.

With the beginnings of a sneer Sharper turned to face the newcomer. His cartridge belt was empty from reloading his Colts. "What can I do for you, mister?" he asked.

Random didn't answer. He stood with his feet planted firmly. His eyes burned like beacons of green fire.

"Well?" Sharper demanded. "I'm askin'. What the hell do you want?"

The blue-coated youth didn't say a word. He didn't need to. The look in his eyes was clear enough.

"I'm tellin' you to clear out," Sharper said, licking his lips. "You can't draw on me."

"I won't draw on you," Random said in a voice as dry as the inside of Cal Sharper's mouth.

"You come to arrest me, Mr. Deputy?" Sharper jeered. His strange wild eyes flicked down at Random's hidden hand. Random had come to kill him, and he knew it. The lousy Mex-lover had his Colt, cocked and locked, held inside his coat.

That was fine by Cal Sharper. He'd drawn on a leveled gun once that day. What had been sauce for Gorman's gander could cook Random's goose as well.

He looked Random square in the eye, then threw himself aside, going for his gun.

The long blue coat opened. Instead of a Colt, the fat stage gun swung out. Both barrels let go at once. Sharper was in mid-leap when the double charge caught him. The shot flung him over the disintegrating bar like a toy.

What landed on the planking behind was scarcely recognizable as human from the waist up.

Jerry Moody lunged forward. Random drew his pistol left-handed across his belly and aimed it at him. The sandy-haired pimply kid stopped with his hand on the butt of his gun. He stared at the black, black muzzle of the revolver. Then he looked past, to the face of the man holding it.

What he saw there was like a sinner's first glimpse of the waiting jaws of hell. He backed away slowly. His hand fell from the gun butt.

When he realized Random would let him go, he ran outside and threw up in the muddy street.

The other two toughs sidled past Random, then bolted out and down the street. When Random stepped from the *cantina* into a fitful rainfall, Tag Carroll was just riding up with three ranchhands.

Carroll jumped off his Appaloosa. "Where's Sharper?" he demanded. When no answer was forthcoming, he strode forward and grabbed hold of Random's coat front.

He gasped and doubled over as Random drove his fist into the rancher's big, soft belly. Carroll sat down in the mud, losing his hat on the way. His face turned purple. His mouth worked, trying to swallow air.

The ranchhands started to come off their horses. "Come ahead," Random told them as he drew his gun. "Do something. Do anything. *Please.*"

Carroll's wranglers took one look at the young man and decided they were going to do nothing. No one else made a move to stop him as he mounted his gray mare and rode off toward the school.

CHAPTER FOURTEEN

Random sat in Sheriff Hoopwright's office in the hide warehouse. The chinless sheriff looked scared. Random felt none too cocky himself.

The thunderstorm had broken for real after Sharper had died the day before. It was a real gully-washer, the heaviest in ten years. The streets of San Rael became all but impassable.

Despite the mud, Tag Carroll had marched to Hoopwright's office to demand Random's arrest for the murder of Cal Sharper. Hoopwright had refused to open the door to the rancher, but he had summoned up the gumption to inform Carroll that Random was his legally empowered deputy and had acted duly in defense of his own life while discharging his duties.

Infuriated, Carroll gathered his own men and Sharper's friends and rode to the schoolhouse with the intent of dispensing some frontier-style justice of his own.

Unfortunately, Carroll had not counted on the possibility that the events of the last twenty-four hours would bring Random's men behind him even more solidly. They were loyal to their young chief, and eight of them met Carroll and his band at the steps of the schoolhouse. At their head was none other than Bob Chase, who firmly told the rancher to take his friends and clear out. In the face of eight cocked Winchesters, the would-be lynchers were none too eager to contest the matter, though Carroll had suffi-

cient bluster left to promise retribution before riding
off through the downpour.

Ultimately, the sole factor that prevented further
outbreaks of violence that day was the torrential rain.
Most of the Anglos backed Random. The young outsider had been doing the job he'd been hired for with
only one setback, and the fact Bob Chase still followed Random after having his own home burned
impressed the townspeople. Also, a lot of folks felt
Cal Sharper was better off dead. But Carroll, Jerry
Moody, and the late gunslinger's other associates were
thirsty for vengeance, and they said so.

While all this went on, Random was fretting and
pacing the floor of the schoolhouse. Time was wast-
ing. He wasn't getting a chance to follow up on what
he'd found out in Los Duranes. None of his men
knew of any Raymond Mason, though one or two
said the name rang a bell. And he couldn't go asking
around because of the rain and because his men
would not allow him out for fear of ambush by Sharper's friends.

That night the patrol stayed in the warm dryness
of the schoolhouse. With the arroyos running bank
high the *gorras* would not be riding. Random offered
to let his men go home, but they decided to stay on.

Just before Random went to bed, Tanner came by.
Shaking water from his hat and dripping the rain
from his yellow rainslick, Tanner told Random that
Sheriff Hoopwright had issued an ultimatum. Any
man making threats against the deputy sheriff of San
Rael would be arrested for disturbing the peace, and
that went for Tag Carroll as much as anybody. Without the rancher having to say so, Random knew the
sheriff had raised the nerve to make such a statement
under pressure from Tanner himself and Clay Barnes,
so Random thanked the iron-haired Tanner and
turned in.

If the long, bloody day ended on a favorable note,

the beginning of the next day more than made up for it.

When he came to see Random in the predawn murk José Pacheco was a badly frightened man. The *nativos* were up in arms about the killing of the child. They were crying for revenge against the *gringo* baby murderers, and *El Jefe* was willing to give it to them.

When darkness fell that night the *gorras blancas* would ride to the other San Rael in a raid that would drive the paleskins clear out of Duran County. The White Hoods could very well have the strength for it, too; recruits had poured in all night despite the thunderstorm.

Nor were all the recruits hotheaded youngsters. A goodly number were older, more sober men, sickened beyond endurance by the slaying of four-year-old Angelina Sanchez.

The war Random had tried so desperately to avert was about to break out with a force to dwarf the storm.

These ugly tidings had Sheriff Hoopwright swallowing his prominent Adam's apple repeatedly and gazing bug-eyed at his deputy. "I'll handle the town's defenses," Random assured him. "Chase and Webb Gordon are making the preparations right now."

He stood up to leave. The smell in the humid corner of the hide warehouse was choking. Then he remembered the question he had been wanting to ask for over twenty-four hours.

"Raymond N. Mason? Can't say's I know him. 'Course, now that you mention it, that name does sound a might familiar. . . . Nope. Can't seem to put my finger on it."

"Keep thinking about it," Random said. "Whether a war starts tonight or not may depend on finding him. I'll be out at the school."

An icy wind was blowing up the Trail from the east. Random turned up his collar against it and stepped off the boardwalk into the river of soupy red-brown mud that was the main thoroughfare this morning.

"Morning, brother," a voice called behind him.

Random looked back up the street. A man was riding through the quagmire with the wind at his back. "Morning," he replied.

"Just down from Los Duranes," the newcomer said. He had *cowhand* written all over him and pronounced the name "Doo-rain-ees," but to Random he was absolutely beautiful. "Got a telegram for a Mr. Random. This here the Sheriff's office? They told me—"

"I'm Random." His heart seemed to be in the base of his throat. Was his luck about to change for the better?

The man fished inside his slicker, produced a folded slip of yellow paper. "Here y'are."

Random reached in his own pocket, brought out a silver dollar. "No thanks," the cowboy said, handing over the telegram. "Pasty-faced sissy of a clerk at Western Union done give me five. Wouldn't be fair to get paid twicet."

Random thanked him and the wrangler rode away whistling tunelessly. Fingers trembling, Random unfolded the telegram and read it. Then he read it again, scrutinizing every word as if expecting the message to change before his eyes.

The door opened behind him. Hoopwright came clomping out onto the boardwalk. "Oh, there you are," the sheriff said. "I finally figgered out who Raymond N. Mason is."

Random looked inquiringly at him. "Didn't recollect at first, on account of nobody ever calls him by his real name. He's known as Slim, mostly. Clay Barnes's cattle boss, up to the high pasture."

Once, during a brief stint as a coaler on a Baltic timber ship, Random had visited the famous Tivoli Gardens in Copenhagen. They had a contraption there where a man could pay to test his strength by hitting a plank with a mallet and catapulting a little ball up a post. If it reached the top it rang a bell. Something similar happened inside the young man's brain just at that moment.

"By any chance, was this Slim Mason the man who brought you that telegram from the Durango marshal—the one about Noe Villareal?"

"Why, it sure enough was."

Random folded the telegram with exaggerated care and stuck it in an inside pocket of his greatcoat. "When you went after Villareal, which way did he head?" he asked.

"Found out later he'd run out on the north road. Goes to Calverton and San Martin, up in the north part of the county. 'Course, we know now he din't go either place."

True, Random thought. *But not the way you're thinking—nor I, till this very moment.*

"You are certain Villareal was warned."

Hoopwright scratched behind one ear. "Musta been the way of it," he said, "unless he's got the second sight. Cut out just as we rode in. But who could have warned him? Don't make no sense at all."

"Oh, it makes sense," Random said. "All the sense in the world." He mounted his mare and spurred her into a slogging lope, and left the sheriff standing with his mouth hanging open.

He found what he was looking for only by the wildest of accidents. The sun had broken through the clouds and lay almost atop the western peaks. Random was cold and drenched through from having buckets of water dumped on him every time his hat brushed an overhanging pine bough.

It was getting late. He was getting desperate. He needed to be back at nightfall to defend San Rael, if he could find no way to avert the raid.

It was a terrible irony in a way. With what he knew now, the entire plot stood revealed in all its

cynical splendor. If he could convey his knowledge to
the warring factions, they would forget their differ-
ences and turn with vengeful fury on the cunning
mastermind behind it.

The only problem was, no one would believe Random's revelations. Not without an almighty lot of
proof. And it was part of that proof he was despair-
ing of locating in time when something peculiar
caught his eye.

There was nothing particularly outstanding about
the five black cows blocking the forest trail that led to
San Martin and Calverton. There was not much unusual about the brown, ten-year-old boy in charge of
them, wrapped in a blanket *poncho* against the ele-
ments. It was the metallic object peeking from one
side of the *ponch* that took Random's interest.

"*Buenos,*" he said to the urchin. The boy gazed at
him with no fear in his shiny black eyes.

"*Buenos días*, señor," he replied courteously.

"That's a very fine *pistola* you have there, *amigo,*"
Random said, hoping the boy understood English.
The child nodded, pleased at the compliment. "May
I see it?"

The boy's curiosity became narrow-eyed wariness.
What did the *gringo* stranger have in mind?

Random produced the coin the Los Duranes man
had turned down. "I will give you this," Random
said, "for only letting me see that marvelous revolver
of yours."

With a calculating expression on his face the boy
pulled the gun out, butt held between thumb and
forefinger. The wooden grips had rotted away. Random dismounted and took the gun in exchange for
the silver dollar.

The gun smelled strongly of wet earth. Random
studied it carefully. It was an enormous cap-and-ball
pistol of outmoded design. He scratched away the
mud crusted on the barrel with a fingernail, revealing
the Colt imprint.

He turned the piece over in his hands. "Where did you find this?" he asked.

The child was immediately filled with indignation. "I did not find it, señor. It was give to me by my father. He say to me, 'Guard well our cattle, Pascualito, for the thieving *gringos*—'"

"Do not lie to me, Pascualito. We are both men of the world here, *qué no?* The gun smells of the ground, not of the oil with which a wise man like your father would protect such a fine weapon. There is sand in the barrel, and black dirt caked around the cylinder. Tell me the truth, where did you find it?"

Pascualito looked stubborn. Random dug in his pockets and produced a double eagle. The fifty dollars' earnest money he'd received from the man in St. Louis was pretty well gone. But if he wanted to collect the other $950 of his fee—if he was ever going to be *alive* to—he had to do something very soon.

"Here," he said, holding up the gold coins where the boy could see it. "Twenty dollars. I will buy this pistol from you for this money, but you must tell me where you found it."

"But, señor, I—"

Random cut off his protest. "Twenty dollars is twice what you would pay for a brand-new pistol. And look, this one is useless. See?" He held it out by the barrel. The cylinder was warped and deeply scored, and the frame was twisted. The piece was useless, smashed beyond repair by the impact of a heavy slug.

The child nodded eagerly and snatched the coin from Random's fingers. Twenty dollars was a fortune, and if all the *gringo* wanted was a broken pistol—!

When the boy fulfilled the second part of his bargain Random's heart fell. "One of my cows, she wander into this arroyo," the boy said, pointing into the wash below the ridge to which he'd led Random, about a hundred yards from the main trail. "I went down after her and the gun, it was lying on the sand, by the bank."

Random groaned. He sat down heavily on a rock and buried his face in his hands. In his mind he could see the heavy Colt, swept along the arroyo by the floodwaters, tumbling over and over for miles. . . .

The big gun had been buried. If only he could have found out where, he might have been able to obtain the eivdence he had to have, to convince Anglo and native alike it would be lunacy to fight, that they were being used by the same ruthless, brilliant schemer. If only—

He stopped. He was being anything but brilliant himself. He brought the gun out of the pocket where he'd thrust it and studied it. Yes, there was dirt on it, rich black dirt like that beneath his feet.

If the gun had been washed downstream by a flash flood the dirt would have been scoured from it.

Random looked up. In the arroyo he could see the jumble of prints in the damp sand, where Pascualito had gone after his cow and turned up an unexpected treasure. His eye climbed the slope of the ridge from that point upwards, tracing the course the pistol might have taken in a downhill slide when rain dislodged it.

Twenty yards away a lordly Ponderosa stood, precariously perched on the very brink of the ridge. The night's violent rainfall had washed black earth away from the downslope side of its base, revealing a tangle of sturdy roots.

Slowly, Random walked to the lone pine. The boy followed two paces behind. They came to the tree and stopped.

"Madre de Díos!" the boy choked, pointing.

From the snarl of tree roots protruded a weathered boot.

Random knelt and scraped away earth. He heard Pascualito cry out again, then turn and run off. He could scarcely blame the boy. The thing he was unearthing was not pretty to look at.

It was a human skeleton, the bones brown and covered here and there with patches of dark, dried skin. Grotesquely, it was fully dressed, though its linen shirt was stained almost black by the soil, and the long frock coat was nearly rotted away.

The leering skull had an extra hole gaping above the vacant, staring eye sockets. With the toe of his boot Random scuffed decomposing cloth from the skeleton's chest. Several of the exposed ribs were scored or broken. By bullets, heavy bullets, like the ones that had plowed into the old Colt, rendering it useless for firing—or even for use as a prop in a grisly masquerade.

The ambushers had taken the surviving pistol, distinctive even without its mate, to help a man assume the identity of the corpse beneath the tree. Not being religious men, or at least not of the same religion as their victim, the killers might have overlooked a certain detail. . . .

Random ran his fingers through the dirt around the neck bones. His hand came up with something dangling from it. It was a tiny, tarnished cross on a chain. By its relatively uncorroded state, Random knew even before he scratched off some of the tarnish with his knife that cross and chain were made of silver.

He stood and slipped the cross into a pocket of his *capote*. With a small, ironic smile on his lips he gazed down at the long-ago-murdered man.

"*Adiós*," he told the skeleton. "Farewell, Señor Villareal."

CHAPTER FIFTEEN

Thanks to the stroke of good fortune, Random now felt he had the evidence he needed to demonstrate what was going on in San Rael. Now he needed to be able to prove the identity of the man responsible. That was going to be extremely hard.

The best solution was to get his hands on *El Jefe*. If Random could publicly unveil the *gorras'* leader, there would be no question of who he was. In addition, the capture of *El Jefe* would probably cause the huge raid planned for tonight to fizzle. For this Random needed help, José Pacheco's help.

The disillusioned *gorra* lived in a tiny adobe east of the native village. Circling wide of the settlement, Random arrived with the dusk.

Standing alone in a rude corral, Pacheco's sorrel whinnied a greeting to Random's mount. Otherwise, the place was still. Random swung down from the saddle. "Pacheco?" he called softly.

There was no reply. Uneasy, Random walked to the door of the house. He rapped on it, and it swung open slightly. "Pacheco?"

Silence and shadows returned his greeting. He drew his pistol and pushed the door open gently.

It took a few seconds for Random's eyes to become accustomed to the gloom of the solitary room. Then he understood why there had been no answer.

The master of the house was home. His limp body swung with his bare feet six inches off the hard-packed dirt floor. A rope was knotted to a roof beam, and the other end had been tied around José Pacheco's neck.

A hand-scrawled note was pinned to his chest. *"Yo soy Judaso,"* it read. I am Judas.

Random's hands shook. It might have been a suicide note, written in a fit of remorse at his betrayal of *las gorras blancas*. But Pacheco had never written it.

Not with his hands tied behind his back.

Eulógio Gonzalez' *casa* was as ominously quiet as the renegade night rider's simpler hut. Random tasted bile at the back of his throat. He had gotten Pacheco murdered. Did he also have the blood of his friend Gonzalez and lovely Elena on his hands?

The color of the sky was deepening, starting to go indigo in the east. Random was abruptly aware of the small sounds and smells that followed a rain: the dripping of water from tree limbs, the aroma of wet earth and greenery. In town Chase and Gordon would be doing their best to organize the settlers to meet the coming attack.

A premonition of danger chilled his backbone. Again, he drew and cocked his revolver. The door to the *patio* was unlatched. He opened it and went in. His booted feet were silent as a stalking panther's on the flagstones. "Señor Gonzalez?" he called. "Elena?" As before, at Pacheco's, he got no response. Revolver at the ready, he stepped forward.

A soft sound came from behind him. Too late he started to turn. White light and thunder exploded in his brain. The last thing he saw was the sandstone flagging spinning dizzily up to meet him.

Random's head was throbbing with a slow black-smith's beat. Outside the shadows had grown only slightly longer, and he knew he hadn't been out long. He was sitting in a straight-backed wooden chair in the *sala*, with his arms behind him. A little experimentation confirmed that they were well bound with coarse rope.

Groaning with the pain movement caused, Random turned his head. Roberto Morales stood near the empty fireplace. He held Random's Peacemaker carelessly in one hand and another stuck in his belt—no doubt the one used to blackjack Random.

"You are awake." Roberto smiled. His teeth were very white in the evening. *"Buenas tardes, gringo."*

It felt as if Random's eyelids were lined with sandpaper. His brain reeled and his stomach churned with nausea. He wondered if he had a concussion. A blow on the head could do funny things to a man.

"Eulógio Gonzalez is away, pleading with his neighbors to listen to him. Elena is with him. They think we can be stopped from driving the *gringos* from our lands—the lands that were ours before the *norteamericano* intruders came. Just as you thought you could stop us."

Random forced mind and eyes to focus. "I came to see you, Roberto," he said. "I hoped Elena could tell me where you were."

"Ah, but you are very friendly with the *señorita, qué no?* So friendly you come to visit her each day." His face twisted suddenly. He stepped forward and slapped Random. Random blinked, bit back vomit. "You have made her forget that she is *nativa*, with your smooth tongue and *gringo* lies. I will make her remember! You will grovel and plead like the *gringo* coward you are, and then you will die."

"Listen, Roberto," Random said, shaking his head. It made his brains slosh like water in a bucket. He came close to blacking out. "You're making a mistake. All the *gorras* are!"

"What are you talking about, *cabrón?*"

"You're being used! By the man you call *El Jefe*. Your homes will be taken from you and a railroad built where they stood, and *las gorras blancas* will be the guilty ones!"

"You are lying!" Roberto shouted. *"Lying!"*

"I am not, damn you! *I need your help!"*

"Cállate!" Roberto snarled, backhanding his prisoner. "Shut up. Or I'll kill you now, *gringo!"*

"You won't ever kill him, Roberto," said a voice from behind him. It was a soft voice, a female voice. And a very deadly sounding voice. Roberto turned. Random forced his head to swivel and tried to peer through the haze that suddenly filled his vision.

Elena Gonzalez took another step into the *sala*. She wore a white shirt and black riding pants. At her hip was Random's shotgun, cocked and leveled straight at Roberto's belly.

"Elena! *Carita—"*

"Drop the gun, Roberto," the girl ordered. *"Andale!"*

Random's pistol clattered to the floor. Elena gestured with the stage gun, and Roberto carefully pulled out his own pistol and let that drop as well. Then he stepped away.

"You are a fool, Roberto," Elena gritted. "You will thank me some day for preventing you from becoming a murderer as well!"

"But, Elena, the *gringo—"*

"Shut up!" Random roared, and winced as the sound reverberated in his head. "Listen to me, you two. There is not much time. Elena, do you want the raid prevented? There is still time to save much bloodshed in both San Raels."

"I will do anything I can to help."

"Then let Roberto take something from my coat pocket. The right one." Watching the cavernous twin mouths of the stage gun, Roberto sidled to Random's side. The shotgun followed him like a faithful dog.

The *nativo* stuck his hand in the pocket. A puzzled look crossed his face. The hand came out holding the big revolver Pascualito had discovered. "But what is this?" he asked, looking at the gun in the uncertain light. A frown crossed his face.

"A Walker Colt. Half a matched pair. This one has been smashed by a rifle bullet."

"It looks just like No—*El Jefe*'s!"

Random nodded. "Ouch," he said. "Very good. Now, reach inside the coat. The paper and the other thing."

With a glance at Elena, Roberto obeyed. The girl craned her neck to see what was happening. The side-by-side never wavered.

The young *gorra*'s hesitant fingers drew out the dulled silver chain and the folded telegram. "This is Noe's crucifix!" he cried. He glared at Random. "How did you steal this? What have you done to *El Jefe*? I'll—"

"I do not believe Elena really wants to blow you in two," Random said quietly, "so I would advise you to take it easy. To answer your questions, I did not steal it, and I have done nothing to *El Jefe*. I took the gun and the cross from a dead man, buried three hundred feet from the trail to San Martín. He looked to have been dead all winter."

"But these—but *El Jefe* has—"

"*El Jefe* has the pistol that was not too badly damaged to salvage when his men murdered Noe Villareal last summer. The killers forgot the crucifix —probably because they were Anglos, and not Catholic."

Elena and Roberto stared at him with their eyes bugged out. "Th-this is madness!" Roberto finally managed to stammer. "Villareal is our leader! I know it!"

"Have you seen his face? The crucifix his dying father gave him? The pair of pistols he was so very proud of?"

"No."

"The real Villareal was set up and knocked down like a target in a shooting gallery. The men who murdered Villareal convinced him that he was wanted by the *gringos* for a crime he didn't commit. He fled

town just ahead of Hoopwright—right into an ambush. He's dead, Roberto. The man you call *El Jefe*
killed him."

"I do not believe it," the young man stated firmly.
"The *gringos* were after him. The marshal in Durango sent a telegram."

"I thought so too," Random said, "till I received
the telegram you've got in your hand. Look at it."

With Elena looking over his shoulder, Roberto unfolded the paper and read:

GUNMAN CONFESSED AUGUST ROBBERY MURDER STOP
DURANGO NEVER HEARD OF VILLAREAL STOP PINKER-
TONS EITHER STOP LUCK STOP KELLY END

Thunderstruck, Roberto looked up. "What does it
mean?" Elena asked.

"I got it this morning. It means that a man named
Slim Mason brought a telegram last summer to Sheriff Hoopwright that purported to be a message from
the marshal in Durango. It was a fake. It was merely
a trick to get Noe Villareal to drop out of sight and
run obligingly into a trap."

"Why?" asked Roberto, dumbfounded.

"So that someone could assume his identity. Your
Jefe, the founder and leader of the San Rael White
Hoods."

Roberto looked at the girl. Her face was blank, un-
comprehending. "*José y María*," he breathed. "Elena,
forgive me! I thought I was doing right!"

"You also thought I was paying court to the girl
when I visited here," Random said, "when in fact I
came to talk with her father. Now cut me loose."
Dumbly Roberto obeyed.

"Why did you want to talk to me?" he asked.

"Pacheco is dead. He was my link to the *gorras*—
that's how I came to be at that gathering north of
your village. You must tell Elena about it someday.

You just paid me back in kind for the rap I gave you that night."

Elena frowned. "Who is he?" Roberto demanded hoarsely. "Who is *El Jefe?* I will kill him!"

"I won't tell you," Random said. "You'd never believe it, and it would do no good. I need to catch him. That is the only way people will believe me."

"I want revenge," Roberto gritted.

"Do you think I don't? This man murdered Luke Cranston and José Pacheco himself, he was responsible for the death of Villareal, and the other killings too—the little girl, Russ Gorman, even Cal Sharper and the two *gorras* who died trying to kill me." Random stood up and took a swaying step forward. "He also made a fool out of everyone in either San Rael—including me."

Elena was at his side. He held her off with the palm of his hand. "I'll live," he said. "But now you have to promise me your help, Roberto. Can you see why the raid must not take place?"

Roberto nodded. "Yes," he said faintly.

CHAPTER SIXTEEN

The Anglo settlement of San Rael was in an uproar. Armed men challenged Random as he rode in past the outskirts of town, but they recognized him and let him pass. None belonged to his militia.

The town itself was a blaze of light. The greatest commotion was at the stables in the very center of town, next to the tanner's yard and the warehouse where the sheriff's office was. The corral was filled with men and horses.

Webb Gordon hailed Random as he rode up. "You've done well," Random told him, "but you'd better send someone to pull in the men north of town. We don't want anybody getting shot by accident." Gordon nodded and relayed the order to a couple of youths standing nearby, who immediately leapt on their ponies and galloped away.

"Any trouble?" Random asked his assistant.

"No." Gordon jerked his head at a guttering torch roped to the corral railing. Random's employers stood there, except Clay Barnes. His back injury was acting up worse than ever, and he had remained in his room all day.

Tag Carroll had a look of triumph on his face and was strutting like a prairie grouse cock in the mating season. "Was afraid Carroll'd want to jump the Mexes before they came for us," Gordon told Random. "But he says he reckons this way's better. Wants to prove once and for all that Mexes can't stand up to white men in a fair fight."

"He may have his chance tonight," Random said. "Get the men mounted and ready to ride. I have word the *gorras* are coming down the middle trail, the west arroyo. Take the men to the place where the lookouts are usually posted and stop. And I mean stop. This is now a military emergency, and military rules apply. If someone disobeys, shoot him. I accept all responsibility."

Squaring his shoulders, he headed toward his employers. His mind was still fuzzy from the blow on the head, but the pain had settled down to a dull throb. Carroll greeted him with a smirk and a hearty clap on the back that sent spears of agony lancing through his skull. "Well, son," the red-faced rancher declared. "Seems you finally come to your senses. You done a fine job gettin' these men into shape. So I'm a-willin' to let bygones be bygones. We can just sort of forget our little misunderstandings."

Fighting an urge to bury his fist in Carroll's belly a second time, Random said, "I'll go along with that, Mr. Carroll. But it's Gordon and Bob Chase who got the men prepared. I was out scouting."

He turned to include the others. "The *gorras* murdered my informant. But I got information anyway. The night riders will come by way of the middle trail on the map. I've just told Gordon to take the men out and get ready for them. I'll have eight or ten stay back in town in case the raiders try any tricks. You'll be staying behind as well."

The men burst into heartfelt protests—though the good sheriff's protests weren't quite as heartfelt as some—but Random stilled them with his hand. "The *gorras* have instructions to shoot any and all of you on sight. They realize how important you are to the defense of this town, and are acting accordingly. I know personal danger won't sway you, but the fact is we cannot afford to lose even one of you." The lie set Random's teeth on edge, at least where Tag Carroll was concerned. Random could have lost him without turning a hair. "It would be best if you gentlemen set up headquarters at the Barnes house. That way you can be reached in an emergency."

"Clay's feelin' badly," Tanner said. "Cain't hardly eat for the pain. Ain't seein' nobody neither—I tried to talk to him earlier. Door's locked tighter'n a mule's asshole in horsefly country. Junella's fit to be tied."

"Miss Barnes will understand," Random said. "That house is the best location."

All around them men were swinging up into the saddles of excited horses. There was a noise like hundreds of metallic crickets as rifles and revolvers were checked. Giving in to Randoms' persuasion, Tanner, Carroll, Bacon, the doctor, and Hoopwright mounted up and headed for the big house overlooking the San Rael Trail. Random climbed aboard his gray, ready to ride out ahead of the body of men.

He sought out Gordon. "Detail ten men to stay behind and keep a watch on the town," he said. "Better send a couple to stand guard at the Barnes place. That's going to be our HQ while this is going on." As Gordon wheeled his horse to comply, Random heard his own name called.

"Hey, Mr. Random," a vaguely familiar voice hailed him. "Over here. It's important." Random looked toward the sound. A wave of sickness hit him from nowhere, but he stayed upright by force of will. At last he was able to make out a skinny shape in the shadow of the warehouse.

"It's me, Freddie," the shape said. "The sheriff's nephew, remember?" Random remembered. Freddie had been taking the notes in Hoopwright's office after Shorty was killed.

"What do you need?" Random asked.

"Out here in the yard, behind the warehouse. A guy from Mextown, says he got to see you. He's hurt real bad."

God, what now? Random thought. If the wounded man proved to be Roberto Morales it would be disastrous. "Take them on ahead," Random yelled to Webb Gordon. "I'll be along shortly. Remember what I told you."

"Yessir!" Gordon replied. "All right, you heroes. Let's ride!"

San Rael seemed to be pretty thick with former sergeants, Random reflected—there was no mistaking the snap in Gordon's voice. Sixty horsemen rolled out of the corral like thunder. Dust boiled into the air to join the reek of kerosene, gun oil, and fresh horse dung. Random looped his reins over the fence and walked from the enclosure, over to the looming bulk of the warehouse.

Freddie retreated into the tanner's yard as Random came forward. "What's the trouble?" Random asked.

The yard was surrounded by a board fence. The long-unused tanner's racks were grotesque black shapes in the light of a single lantern. "Trouble for you, mister," a man said. "Hold it right there."

Four men appeared out of the darkness. Random heard Freddie's boot heels as he ran for safety—having collected his thirty pieces of silver in advance, Random reckoned. "Good evening, Slim," he said pleasantly to the tallest and oldest of the four. "Or should I say, Mr. Mason? It's hard to recognize you without a kerchief tied over your face."

At a gesture from the old Henry rifle Random raised his hands. "Jerry here's real unhappy with you for killin' his pal," Slim said, nodding at the slender youth beside him. "We got together with these two—" he moved his head to indicate the two cowhands flanking him and Moody "—to sort of teach you not to stick your nose in things what don't concern you none."

"I'm being paid to stick my nose in," Random said. "Why don't you tell Jerry what you're really worried about? Worried that even now I'll find some way to head off the big battle tonight and spoil the plans you helped put into action."

"What's he talkin' about, Slim?" Jerry Moody asked.

"Nothin'," Slim drawled, glancing nervously at the youth. "Just trying to trick you, thass all. He's one smooth-talkin' feller, all right."

"I'm that," Random agreed cheerfully. The fog in his brain had evaporated miraculously. His headache was gone. He had walked open-eyed into a trap that could finish him, but the excitement of danger that thrilled in his veins was making him feel fully alive again. "If you'll just listen, Jerry, I'll tell you who warned Villareal that the sheriff was looking for him—by coincidence, he's the same man who brought the telegram that started Hoopwright after him in the first—"

"*Shut up!*" roared the rangy cowhand. The quartet closed in menacingly. "Or we'll shut your mouth for you."

"You've had me on the down side of four-to-one odds before, Slim," Random reminded him. "It didn't work out very well, did it?"

Moody wasn't showing a weapon, but the two nameless cowboys had their Winchesters leveled. Their fingers tightened on the triggers. "Don't say another word," Slim said, stepping up to Random, "and you might, just only might, live to see the sun come up." For emphasis he jabbed Random with the muzzle of the repeater, the way he'd jabbed the captive Gonzalez not many days ago.

It was a mistake. Random's hands, unlike the little round *nativo*'s, were not tied. And while, like most Westerners, Slim thought of a rifle as a weapon to be fired or used as a rather clumsy club, in the hands of a French Foreign Legionnaire a rifle was nearly as deadly empty as loaded.

Random's expression never changed from a rueful grin. He plucked the Henry from Slim's fingers by the barrel, turning his body away from the lethal gape of the muzzle. The butt swung up and slammed into the pit of the wranglers' stomach.

Slim doubled over, gagging. The man on Random's extreme left was still standing and gaping when the Henry smashed across the bridge of his nose. He fell back streaming blood as Random struck the rifle from the other cowboy's hand and drove the steel butt plate of Slim's gun into his groin. The man screamed shrilly and collapsed.

Jerry Moody had his revolver out. He fired wildly as Random rushed him. The shot went by Random's ear and he brought the rifle barrel down on Moody's forearms. Bones cracked. Moody cried out, then crumpled when Random hit him on the side of the head.

Behind Random, the man with the broken nose had recovered and, rifle to shoulder, was trying to get a bead on him through a red haze of agony. Random whirled like a tiger, knocked the rifle spinning from the man's grasp, and poked him hard in the throat with the Henry's muzzle.

His breath regained, Slim uncurled and made a dive for the abandoned Winchester as its owner went down choking. His fingers touched the wooden stock, and then the butt of his own Henry smashed his fingers into the packed earth.

Slim raised his head. Yellow light splintered off the butt plate of the upraised rifle. The glow from the overturned lantern made Random's face a twisted demonic mask.

"God! *Nooo*—!" Slim shrieked. The rifle crashed into his skull.

The fight was over. Random tossed the Henry into a corner of the yard, then surveyed the carnage. Jerry Moody was unconscious in the middle of the tanner's yard. At his side the broken-nosed cowhand breathed heavily through a damaged windpipe. The other unidentified cowpoke was coiled tightly about himself, mewling like a lost kitten with pain.

The fighting fury subsided. *Fools!* Random

thought. *Overconfident fools*. The sickness was coming back.

The gray shied when she smelled the blood spattered over his coat. "Easy, beauty," he told her, holding her by the bridle and patting her nose. The soft words seemed to soothe her. Random put a foot in the stirrup and hauled himself up. Suddenly dizzy, he overbalanced and had to clutch the saddle horn to keep from falling.

Got to hold on, he told himself. *Can't let myself go under*. His field of vision expanded and contracted with his heartbeat as he spurred on the trail of his sixty riders.

CHAPTER SEVENTEEN

Following orders, Gordon had stopped the horsemen at the lookout over the arroyo trail. The cool, clean night air had cleared Random's head somewhat by the time he reached the rearmost members of the party. They waved and grinned to him, confident and collected, glad at the chance of striking back at the raiders who'd tormented them for months.

If Random had any say in the matter, they wouldn't have that chance after all.

At the head of the column Gordon was talking softly with Chase and Bruce MacCaleb, whose bandaged arm was not bothering him enough to keep him out of this night's action. "What was that about, back at the warehouse?" Gordon asked his chief as Random rode up.

"Nothing. False alarm."

"Jesus *kee-rist!*" Sherman whistled. "You look like you been in a landslide. What the hell happened?"

Random glanced down at his bloody coat front. "Ran into a low-hanging tree limb. Bloodied my nose." It made him look clumsy, but not as clumsy as he felt. He had walked into two traps that day, not an impressive record for a professional soldier. He had survived them both, granted. But his luck couldn't hold out forever if he kept walking into the snares his enemies set for him.

He fished out his watch and squinted at it. The moon was better than half full, so that he had little trouble reading the time. "The *gorras* should be along in half an hour," he said. "It looks as if you've got things well in hand here, so I'm going to ride ahead and watch for them—see if I can give you a little advance warning."

"It's risky," MacCaleb said. "They'll be looking for trouble and hot on the trigger."

"If you hear gunfire, I'll probably be able to use all the help I can get," Random said. "Otherwise I'll slip back to your position when I spot the raiders."

In the moonlight Random easily found the spot he and Roberto had agreed upon. It was a broad clear space in the woods, cut across by the arroyo. He stationed himself in the trees on its southern edge, drew the Vetterli from its boot, and sat down to wait.

Not so long ago Random would have called Roberto a liar for telling him the raid was coming by way of the wash. It was known to the Anglos, and to take it would be to invite them to ambush the *gorras*. *El Jefe* was certainly too canny a leader for that.

But then, not so long ago, Random would not have known that the counterfeit Villareal would *want* his raiders to ride into an ambush. That he wanted a pitched gun battle to take place. The bloodier, the better.

Random's mouth was dry. There was still some water in the canteen he carried by his saddle, and it was cool and refreshing when he drank it off. He was just lowering the emptied container when he heard the sounds.

The muffled thud of horses' hooves on sand drifted down the arroyo. Back in the forest, Random's mare lifted her head, and he was glad he'd remembered to wrap her nose, to muffle any fatal whinny to the mounts of the approaching *gorras*. He was still feeling the effects of the clout Roberto had given him, and was afraid he would overlook some important detail like that, which could cost him dearly.

Suddenly they were there. From bank to bank the wash was filled with white-hooded riders. Others rode the banks, spreading out to avoid jostling each other into the arroyo.

On the left bank was a well-remembered figure on a tall, dark horse. The frock coat was open and a massive, gleaming pistol was thrust through the man's belt. The weapon was in far better shape than its mate, which rode shattered and corroded in the pocket of Random's *capote*.

It was a ghostly, powerful sight. The mass of men rode unspeaking, faceless in their hoods. They had an air of grim purpose, riding beneath the moon like shrouded legions of the night.

From the rear of the raiding party a rider galloped. He slowed his mount alongside the high-stepping black. *El Jefe*'s hooded head turned, nodded. At his signal, the four *gorras* who rode in attendance with him continued straight on, toward the Anglo settlement, and the waiting ambush that *El Jefe* knew lay ahead.

Random nodded with satisfaction. All was going according to plan. Roberto would now lure his leader to one side, pleading some emergency that it would not do to discuss in the midst of the band of raiders. Once there, he would draw his pistol and take *El Jefe* prisoner, spiriting him into the depths of the forest while Random's big Vetterli created a diversion. Bereft of their leader and suddenly under attack by unseen forces, the night riders would, he hoped, turn and run. There was nothing like a violently unexpected turn of events to break even the strongest resolve—especially at night.

However, Random was disregarding once more his own distrust of plans laid in advance. And he was also disregarding the fact that Roberto Morales was a confirmed hothead, with more fire than sense.

Rather than trying to get *El Jefe* off by the trees, Roberto grabbed hold of his sleeve and began yelling at the top of his lungs. Random's Spanish vocabulary was still not exhaustive, but he knew what was happening when the youth started screeching *"Pérfido! Pérfido!"*—traitor, traitor. Rather than doing things Random's way as agreed, Roberto had not been able to resist denouncing the impostor to the entire force of night riders.

It was a very foolish thing for young Morales to do. Random hurt with the sure knowledge of what would come next. One moment the hooded Roberto was gesticulating madly and crying for attention, and then a yard-long flame licked from the tall rider's side and the youth was flying through the air, off his rearing stallion.

What the gunsmith in Los Duranes had said about the Walker being a lot of gun was dead right. *El Jefe*'s pistol had a boom like a fieldpiece, echoing round and round the clearing as hooded heads turned toward the disturbance.

With a sigh, Random slipped a round into the chamber of the Vetterli. A *gorra* passed between him and *El Jefe*. He considered briefly, then fired. The *gorra*'s horse went down as if poleaxed.

The raider chieftain's bodyguards were turning back to deal with the injured Roberto. A second ball from the Vetterli knocked down one of their horses. Startled, the other three scattered. Random put a shot into a pinto clear across the clearing. As he hoped, the undisciplined raiders were firing in all directions now, spoiling their own night vision and making it impossible to tell from where Random's shots were coming.

A horse reared and screamed in panic as its rider fought to drag it away from the brink of the arroyo, and Random's next shot knocked horse and horseman into the wash. Bullets were cutting the undergrowth around the former Legionnaire, as he got up and ran, trying to get closer to Roberto.

He circled the outskirts of the clearing. Horses were shrieking with pain. He grimaced at the sound.

Part of his plan was working out, all right—the

whole army of hooded raiders was in complete confusion. By the inert form of Roberto, *El Jefe*'s high-spirited black was high-stepping in fear, rolling its eyes and whinnying. Random stopped and raised his rifle. He had a clear shot at the head *gorra*.

Something moved on the ground. A man on foot was poised over Roberto, and moonlight gleamed from his knife. It was the bodyguard whose horse Random had shot, come to finish the job his leader was too busy to attend to.

Random's shot knocked him sprawling, and then the black horse was under control and the heavy Walker was coming to bear on the helpless youth, who was stirring feebly almost at the horse's feet.

With no time to aim, Random worked the bolt and fired. *El Jefe* jerked and swayed in the saddle. In the moonlight and against the black coat Random couldn't see where his bullet had struck. But he knew instinctively that the wound wasn't mortal, as *El Jefe* wheeled his horse and fled into the forest.

When the *gorras* saw their leader run away, their morale broke completely. Random knocked down two more horses as a number of riders followed *El Jefe*'s lead. He could now hear the cries of the Anglos riding—so they thought—to the rescue.

The night riders heard them too. It was the final straw. The clearing emptied, the last of the *gorras* just fading into the trees when the whooping settlers broke into the clearing.

Random ran into the open, waving his rifle. Since he wasn't wearing the telltale hood of the *gorras*, no one fired at him. Someone called his name. "Go back!" he responded. "Back! This was a feint, a fake. The real attack is coming from the west, up the Trail!"

The riders reined in. "Go back to town before it's too late!" Random shouted. "They may hit any minute!"

In the heat of the moment no one questioned him. No one had seen the huge party of *gorras* that had filled the clearing seconds before. All anyone had seen were the backs of a few frightened stragglers hightailing for home. As quickly as was possible the Anglos got turned around, thundering back the way they came with their blood pounding at this first success in turning back a "feint."

Roberto was conscious when Random got back to his side. The ball had gone through his chest. He had lost a lot of blood in the *caliche*, but the bullet didn't seem to have punctured a lung.

"Señor . . . Random," the black-haired youth's voice greeted him weakly. "I . . . am sorry. I could not help myself. This man—ahh! This man betrayed my people."

"Don't talk. You're badly hurt and we need to get you to help." Random gently pulled off the mask. Roberto was ashen underneath.

"*El Jefe*—did you—?"

"He got away." Roberto closed his eyes.

Random ran back and brought the mare over. "This'll hurt," he warned the injured man. Then he stooped to take him in his arms.

Elena had done her part of the night's work. The house was brightly lit when Random got there, and the *sala* was full of natives. According to instructions, Elena had rounded up as many adult *nativos* as she could, and brought them to her father's house to hear her presentation of what Random had told her that afternoon. Most of them were landowners and fathers of families, like Eulógio Gonzalez himself. But there were some *viejos* as well, and not one of the younger men.

Heads turned as the door of the *sala* crashed open. Random stood there. Roberto hung in his arms, limp and bloody.

"Buenas noches," Random said stonily. "Here is Roberto Morales. *El Jefe* himself gunned him down in cold blood. If you are done talking, the time has come to act."

CHAPTER EIGHTEEN

The lights were also on at Clay Barnes's impressive manor on the hillside above San Rael. Two men stood on guard duty on the front porch. They peered into the dark and then called out cheerfully as Random rode up.

"Hey there, Mr. Random! Looks like you brought us back some chilibellies."

"That I did, Frank." He glanced back at the four *nativos* sitting their horses sullenly, their wrists tied before them. The reins of each horse were tied to the saddle of the one ahead, with Random holding the reins of the foremost. "I caught them sneaking through the woods north of town."

Frank and his partner were local Anglos, not members of Random's militia. If it struck either as odd that one of the four was a giant, grizzled oldster with a snowy white beard, neither said anything. "Bob Chase and ol' Gordon rode through here with the others a while back," Frank said. "Yelled to us the greasers were circlin', comin' to hit us up the Trail. Ain't heard nothin' since."

"They might have been mistaken," Random said. He dropped to the ground and produced his big shotgun, cocking both barrels. "These men say it was the main attack we turned back. The *gorras* just didn't have the courage to stand up to our boys. Come on, you, we're going inside."

The native men swung their legs over and dismounted. Random kept the shotgun aimed at them.

Frank hammered on the door. It opened. The four captives trudged into the house without a word. The other guard threw Random a mock salute as he passed. Random returned it with a peculiar wolfish grin.

Henry Bacon closed the door behind him. He went past Random and the prisoners into the sitting room. "Random's back," the dimunitive rancher said. "Brought us a whole passel of Mexes, trussed up pretty as you please."

He turned with a smile of approval on his face. The smile froze as he saw the yawning mouth of Random's shotgun that had come to bear on the center button of his brown vest. The *nativos* had been trussed prettily indeed, but the thick hairy ropes around their arms had not been tied too securely. They had slipped off easily, freeing the men's hands to draw concealed pistols. In the hall, beside the stairway, the natives were invisible to the men gathered in the sitting room waiting to see the captives.

"Be careful now, Mr. Bacon," Random cautioned softly. He stepped forward and backed the man at gunpoint into the parlor. Random's employers looked up expectantly, then sat stunned, statuelike. "Take a seat, please."

Eulógio Gonzalez, looking unhappy but determined, held a brace of cocked Colts, as did two of his comrades, one stocky, the other tall and refined in appearance. The fourth man was the ancient patriarch Juan Romero, who had a Colt in one gnarled fist and a mammoth flintlock in the other.

There was never a chance that the San Rael landowners would put up a fight. Random's side-by-side shotgun alone could have turned the room into a lifeless, bloody slaughterhouse. It was Tanner who found his voice first.

"I hope you know what you're doing, son," he said quietly.

"I do."

"What the hell do you think you're doing you . . . you *traitor!*" Carroll burst out. "What makes you think you'll get away with—" The flow of words choked off as the smooth bores of the shotgun swung to stare him in the eye.

"This does, Mr. Carroll. Satisfied?" Sweat ran down Carroll's forehead, but his hands remained glued to the arms of his chair. If he so much as reached for a handkerchief the young mercenary might get the wrong idea. The beefy man recalled what had become of his friend Cal Sharper.

"Have you met my friends? Eulógio Gonzalez, whose life I saved the day before I rode into your town. He was about to be lynched by Slim Mason, Cal Sharper, Shorty Kring, and Jerry Moody when I intervened."

The Anglos goggled at him. "This is Pedro Sanchez—no relation to the girl Sharper murdered. And this elderly gentleman with the magnificent head of hair is Juan Romero. He speaks no English, by the way. So if you do anything to make him nervous he might let off that ancient horse pistol before you get a chance to explain to him you didn't mean anything by it." He smiled. It was not a pleasant smile.

He nodded at the distinguished-looking native. "Finally, this is Ricardo Morales. His son Roberto was a *gorra blanca* until this afternoon. When young Roberto learned what I'm about to tell you, he agreed to help me stop tonight's raid, and all raids from now on." The smile went away. "For his troubles, Señor Morales' son was gunned down by the leader of the night riders."

His audience was listening, that was for sure. They reminded Random of a man in a desert, squinting at a mirage to see if it would go away. Tanner, Carroll, and the others looked as if they particularly hoped Random and his cohorts would fade away like a mirage, if they stared hard enough.

Junella Barnes swept into the room with Lacey behind her. The black girl held a tray of refreshments, which she dropped with a screech of fear as Sanchez aimed his guns at her. Junella turned pale. "What are these filthy Mex—my *God!* What are you *doing?* Mr. Random!"

"I am trying to explain matters to these gentlemen."

Junella's gaze flashed around the room. "You—you've sold out! You traitor! You've sold your own people out to Villareal."

"No, Junella," Random said gently. "I haven't. I couldn't if I wished to. Noe Villareal is dead."

"Y-you killed him? Tonight?"

Random shook his head. "No. He has been dead since last summer, since Sheriff Hoopwright rode after him in the Mexican village. He was murdered, killed by the man who has been calling himself *El Jefe.*"

Junella collapsed into a chair. Random dug one-handed into his capacious pockets, producing the crucifix, the ruined Walker, and, at last, the crumpled telegram. He tossed that onto a low table in front of Hoopwright.

"Read that," he told the sheriff. "It comes from a man of my acquaintance who is very high in the ranks of the Pinkertons. When we've finished here, you are free to confirm it."

With palsied fingers, Hoopwright picked up the piece of paper and held it to his eyes. When he finished reading it his hands were shaking so badly that it fluttered away from him and dropped to the rich carpeting. "Wh-what does it *mean?*" he whispered.

"Well, Sheriff, if you'll just lean forward *very* slowly and pick it up, the other gentlemen can peruse it at their leisure while I tell you a little story."

It took Random the better part of an hour to tell, leaving nothing out, from his rescue of Gonzalez, up through his journey to the county seat and what he'd learned there; the dealings with Pacheco; the discovery of Villareal's corpse and the reasons he went looking for it; the attempt Moody, Mason, and the other two cowhands had made on his life that evening; and, finally, the abortive capture attempt on the leader of the *gorras*, and how Random had managed to wing him before he escaped into the woods. When he was through, the others were gazing at him with varying degrees of understanding or uncomprehension on their faces. Even Tag Carroll looked interested.

Junella, however, sat on the edge of her chair, her lovely face taut and hostile. Her mind was closed. But then, it always was, wherever the *nativos* were concerned. Random had known it would be this way and his heart was saddened. But this was his job, and his heart did not enter into it.

Dr. Stern was the first to collect himself enough to ask an intelligent question. "Why are you so certain there is a plot? I know Slim Mason only indifferently, but like his late friend Shorty he has a very vocal dislike for the natives. Could he not have been acting on his own in this?"

"If he was, then who has been playing the role of *El Jefe*? It was no ghost I shot tonight. Slim was the one who brought the sheriff that counterfeit telegram that sent him after Villareal, and I infer that he was also the one who rode out to let Villareal know he was being hunted. In the heat of the moment, with imprisonment and possible death—for a crime he didn't commit, but could an 'uppity greaser' like Villareal convince a jury of Anglos of that?—coming on Slim's heels, Villareal probably didn't pause to wonder why a Mex-hater like Slim was doing him a favor. So he ran north as Hoopwright came up from the south, straight into a volley of rifle bullets."

Dr. Stern conceded the point with a shrug. He still looked skeptical. "There is another point. Since I started operating, there have been little unexplained leaks of information. For example, how did Cal Sharper know I was in touch with some of the natives? How did *El Jefe* know I was at that meeting of the *gorras?* How did the *gorra* riflemen know I was going to be riding the trail from Los Duranes three days ago? The only men who had access to this information were you, my employers."

"Why, I never heard about that foolishness at the *gorra* meeting till after it happened!" Carroll protested. "You sayin' that one of us told *El Jefe* what you were goin' to do?"

"No," Random said. "Can't you see? I'm saying one of you is *El Jefe.*"

Random barely suppressed a laugh at the expressions on the others' faces. They were looking at him as if he'd suddenly sprouted a rack of antlers like a bull elk. "Now you see why I have you sitting here at gunpoint," he said. "That's the only way I could even begin to make you listen to me."

"But what are you saying?" squeaked Bacon. "O-one of *us?* The *leader* of those damned Mex raiders? You're out of your head."

"Not at all. Think about it. Who else but an Anglo could arrange that little charade with the telegram? You think Slim Mason would have helped a native get Villareal out of the way so he could take his place?" The men could find no answer to Random's questions. "And, finally, who could get Slim to do these things at all? There was a lot of work involved. He had to file that lawsuit in Los Duranes to scare the Mexicans. And, night before last, he had to make sure that the *gorras blancas* could get safely across the high meadow to make their attack—an attack on the house of one of my men. Who, but someone paying Mr. Mason a goodly sum of money."

Random shrugged his shoulders, trying to ease his aching back muscles. The stage gun was beginning to feel as if it were cast lead. "Yes, gentlemen. *El Jefe* is one of your number. An influential man who has the confidence of the community, so as to be above suspicion. A man with a fluent command of the local brand of Spanish, in order to be able to mimic the speech of the native he was impersonating. And, finally, a man with a sound, unimpeachable excuse for being out of sight for long periods of time, most often at night, but sometimes during the day as well. Mr. Carroll—"

The man's formally florid face went the color of a fish's belly. He opened his mouth, but no sound came out.

Random smiled at his discomfiture. "I'm only using you as an example, sir. I would be willing to bet that, on the night I attended the meeting of the *gorras*, you were at home with your family—you have a family, have you not? And I'll wager they could testify to it in court."

Dumbly Carroll nodded. "Perhaps the rest of you have alibis too. Mr. Bacon, for instance, or—"

"Ain't you forgettin' something, son?"

It was the big, rawboned Tanner. "I'd be obliged to know what it is, Mr. Tanner."

"This evenin'," Tanner said, in his deliberate way of talking, "all of us—your employers, like you say— we were right here, talkin' and drinkin', since you left. So that means none of us is this *El Jefe* of your'n."

Random looked surprised. "Did I ever say one of you *in this room?*" He paused to let that sink in. "Before we continue our discussion, I think we should consult with our gracious host, Mr. Clayton Barnes."

It finally hit Junella. With a shriek she launched herself at Random, hands outstretched, curved into talons to claw out his eyes. Sanchez threw his arms around her, guns and all. She fought him wildly while the men cringed away from the wildly swinging muzzles of the guns.

"No!" the girl screamed. "*Nooooo!* Uncle Clay is sick! He's a sick man! Don't listen, it's all a lie. Tell him, Dr. Stern! Tell him Uncle Clay is *sick!*"

"A back injury, Dr. Stern. Recurrent pains—*so he claims.* Is there any way to tell if he's really in pain or not?"

Stern took off his spectacles and wiped them on his cravat. He was ashen. "Now just a minute!" Tag Carroll burst out. "This is plain ridiculous! If Clay had been gallivanting in and out, we'd of seen him!"

"Really? Can you see the stairs from where you're sitting, Mr. Carroll? Can any of you gentlemen?"

"Are you going to listen to this traitor?" Junella cried. Her blue eyes looked an appeal at every man in the room. None would meet her gaze. "How can you call yourselves white men, crawling to a pack of yellow-bellied Mexicans?"

For the first time she became aware of who was holding her. "Let me go this minute you . . . you *greaser!*" she hissed.

Looking stricken, Sanchez glanced at Random. The youth nodded and Sanchez stepped back, releasing the girl. The others heaved a sigh of relief. Those Colts were still cocked.

"There's men all around this house, Mr. Random," Bacon objected. "How could he of got in?"

"There are no men surrounding the house. There are two, in front. I suspect the stairs are not the route he usually uses—a rope ladder could let him in without alerting the household. But he's wounded."

"I think we better do like Mr. Random says, Junella," Tanner said. "I ain't sayin' as I believe him, but I surely would like to hear what your uncle has to say, right about now."

"Mr. Tanner, Mr. Carroll—if you will accompany me?" Random nodded at Gonzalez. "And you as well, señor, if you please. Señor Morales will entertain the rest of you while we have a word with Mr. Barnes."

The three men and Random left the room. Again Random regretted having to involve Gonzalez. But he needed a dependable ally. And his friend was bearing up well. He might not look rugged, but he had shown over and over that he was not lacking in sheer physical courage.

Coattails slapping the backs of his thighs, Random mounted the landing at the top of the stairway. The group halted before a closed door. Light shone from beneath it. Tanner glanced at the roly-poly Gonzalez and rapped on the door with a heavy, weather-beaten fist.

"Mr. Barnes?" he called. "Lucius Tanner. Me and some men'd like to ask you a few questions, sir."

"Can't . . . talk," a voice quavered. "My back— the pain! Can't get my breath."

Junella came flying up the stairs in a swirl of taffeta. She elbowed the men aside and fell against the door. "Uncle Clay," she cried. "Tell them to go away! Tell them to get out of your house!"

Tanner grabbed the girl by the shoulders. He pulled her back. She fought him for a second, then collapsed sobbing against his broad chest. Tanner's eyes promised to deal with Random if the young man's bizarre assertions proved false.

Random tried the door. It was locked. He let in the hammer of his shotgun to avoid an accident, and kicked the door with a booted foot. Junella screamed. Random kicked again, putting his weight behind it. He felt something give. On the third kick there was a tearing of metal and the door swung open.

The men burst into Barnes's bedroom. A single lamp at the bedside gave a wan glow. Clay Barnes was sitting up in his four-poster bed. His face was drained of blood and color. He was wearing the purple gown.

"Oh, Uncle Clay!" Junella sobbed, throwing herself on him. She hugged him fiercely. "Go away! Leave him alone. *Can't you see he's sick?*"

They didn't seem to hear. They were standing and staring right through her.

The robe had slipped from Barnes's left shoulder.

Junella's body tensed convulsively. She pulled away from her guardian, gaping at her hands.

There was blood on them, bright fresh blood. "You're hurt!" she gasped. "You—you've been shot! H-how—?"

For a man with a back injury, Clay Barnes moved fast. In an instant his wounded arm was wrapped around his niece's waist, his face twisted in agony, while his good hand pressed a massive percussion revolver into the mass of honey-colored hair.

There was nothing anyone could have done. The others were too startled to react, and Random, who had known what he would find in the room, was helpless. If he fired his weapon, the buckshot charge would kill the girl.

"Clay—" Carroll began, stepping forward.

Barnes ground the Walker painfully against the girl's temple. Her blue eyes were wide with shock. "Don't take another step!" he snarled. "Drop those guns, or the girl is dead."

With a sigh of disgust, Random threw the uncocked stage gun away from him. That made three traps he'd walked into that day. He was one hell of a soldier.

Gonzalez let in the hammers of the Colts he'd borrowed from his neighbors and dropped the guns. "Gun belts too," Barnes said. He was obeyed with careful movements.

"Why, Clay?" Tanner asked. "Why did you do it?"

Barnes winced as a stab of pain went through his shoulder. "To get it back. They stole it from me, and I had to get it back!"

"What are you talking about, Clay?" Tanner's face showed pain. "Who stole it? Stole what?"

"You could never understand!" Barnes hissed. His face was contorted with emotion. "I built that railroad by myself. It was an empire, spanning this continent, and it was mine. But they took it from me!"

He spat. "What do you know about it? How can

you understand? How pathetic it's been, watching you comic, silly little people scrap and struggle for your pitiful plots of land. My own board of directors robbed me of something immeasurably more valuable—and they didn't use guns, oh no. Proxies, dummy corporations, plain bribery—weapons too subtle for the likes of you, but more powerful than any gun!"

"So you were going to force them to give you back your position with the company," Random said dully, "with the San Rael right-of-way as your leverage."

"You're so damned clever."

"But you was the one suggested hiring Random in the first place," Carroll said. "Why'd you do that, if you were in back of . . . all this?"

"*Camouflage*, as Random's French friends would say. I was the only man in San Rael with any suggestions of how you could protect your precious mud homes. Who'd think I had anything to do with the raids?" He glared at the youth in the long blue coat. "I wish Shorty had done the job I sent him to, that day."

"He couldn't, nor could Slim this evening. Nor Cal Sharper. Poor Cal never knew how you used him. He didn't know Slim and Shorty were in on the secret of the night riders. Never knew the reason they wanted to lynch Señor Gonzalez was to increase the hatred between the settlements of San Rael. 'Where's Villareal'—if that poor dumb gunslinging bastard had only known!"

"That's enough," Barnes said. "Back on down the stairs. Tell whoever's down there they're not to try anything cute." With a tremendous effort he hauled himself and the girl off the bed. Junella came along limply. Her entire world had just crashed into ruins. She was dazed.

Gonzalez fired a fast stream of Spanish as they backed down the steps. The natives dropped their guns. When the four reached the bottom Barnes gestured them back.

Keeping his white-faced ward between him and the rest Barnes staggered down into the foyer. Lacey gave a little cry and fainted. "Don't try to follow me," Barnes warned. "If you do, she dies."

He went out the door. They heard him snarling at the two sentries, and an instant later, the thump of weapons falling on the porch. Random dashed past the astounded men, Anglos and natives both, and through the hall.

He exploded onto the porch. Barnes was in the yard, backing away from the house. He was trying to get to a horse, but the tethered beasts sensed something was wrong, and kept sidling away from him.

"Bring me a horse!" he ordered Random when the youth appeared. "Bring one over to me, nice and slowly."

Random walked down the steps, across the yard to his gray mare. His eyes never left the rancher and his hostage. Junella kept trying to look back at the gun pressed to her head. She pleaded constantly for her uncle to come to his senses, let her go, tell her this was just a bad dream—to comfort her the way he used to. He didn't seem to hear.

"You're smart, kid," Barnes told Random with a smile of triumph. "But you won't stop me now."

With one smooth motion Random had the Vetterli out of its scabbard. Barnes ducked down behind his ward as the muzzle came up. "You're bluffing!" he called. "You won't! You can't hit me without hitting the girl." He peered over Junella's shoulder. Random was drawing a bead on his head as though deaf to the warning.

Barnes hunched down again, shielding his head with Junella's body. "Don't do it!" someone yelled from the porch, onto which the men had spilled from the house.

The Vetterli's barrel dropped and spat flame.

Clay Barnes bellowed as his right leg was knocked out from under him by the bullet. The Walker Colt spun end over end and disappeared in the darkness. Junella folded to the ground and lay still.

Random was first at her side. Others came running as he knelt down. She was untouched. He stood back up.

On the ground five yards away Barnes had rolled onto his side and was trying to drag himself away. Anglos and natives clustered about him. Blood was welling from a hole in his thigh.

"If you're going to hide behind a woman's skirts, Mr. Barnes," Random said, "then you shouldn't let your leg stick out."

"You should have killed me, Random," Barnes gasped as strong hands lifted him. "I'll get you for this. No matter what."

The doctor was at Junella's side. "She'll be all right," he declared, getting back to his feet. Random nodded. A knot of men was carrying the twice-wounded Barnes to his porch.

"Barnes was right, you know," Stern said. "He may be convicted and sent to jail, but he's got a lot of money and influence. He'll make trouble for you." Random looked at him, unspeaking.

The man called Frank came running up. "Doc, you better come," he said breathlessly. "Somethin's funny with Cl—with Mr. Barnes."

"Is it the pain?"

"Naw." Frank shook his head. "Hell, that's what's odd. He just nodded off to sleep, a second ago."

"Sleep?" The doctor looked puzzled. "Well, of course, he may be in shock." He hurried off toward the porch. Random stayed where he was, kneeling once more to cradle the unconscious girl in his arms.

In a moment Stern was back. "The ball smashed the femoral artery, Mr. Random," he said quietly. "With such a wound there is nothing an attending physician can do. Clay Barnes bled to death in a matter of a few heartbeats. Chance, Mr. Random?"

Random shrugged. "I was hired by the people of San Rael to do a job," he reminded the doctor. "Now it's done."

CHAPTER NINETEEN

"There was a rope ladder in a locked trunk in Barnes's room," Random told his hosts over lunch. "It turned out he didn't use it very often, though. The servant girl, Lacey, has admitted to helping him sneak in and out of the house on occasion. She even helped him get in that last night. Made a big show of serving refreshments while he slipped up the stairs."

He sipped his coffee. "In the same trunk we found a stack of papers—legal documents, correspondence. Apparently Mr. Clay Barnes was founder and once chairman of the board of directors of the Western Rail Corporation. He got eased out by some kind of trickery I'm a long way from understanding. Left him with a lot of money but no power, no say in his own corporation. Made him bitter. He came out here in humiliation, and twelve years later an opportunity to get his own back was dropped in his lap."

Random reached into a pocket of his jeans. "There was also this in the trunk," he said, laying something among the dishes on the table.

"Una gorra blanca," Eulógio Gonzalez said. "A white hood. All was as you said it was." He shook his head.

"Why did Mr. Barnes try to kill you, señor?" Roberto Morales asked. He was thinner and much less intense than when Random first encountered him. His chest was wrapped tightly in bandages. *El Jefe's* stolen Walker had broken ribs but missed doing any permanent damage. "He hired you to come here—it was his idea, *qué no?* If he wanted to cover up what he was doing by hiring you, why did he send Shorty and Slim and the—the *gorras* to kill you?"

"I suppose I was digging too close to the truth. When he first realized how much I was learning in the *nativo* community, he sent Shorty after me. When I came back from Los Duranes he knew I would have learned that something more was going on in this corner of Duran County than a little idiotic night riding, and had some of his *gorra* thugs waylay me." Roberto winced at this choice of words. "Finally, he tried to have me taken out of the picture before that last big raid. He knew I'd be trying to head it off and was afraid I'd succeed. Which I did, after a fashion."

All was quiet for a time. Joselito came in and cleared off the table. "Well, all's well that ends," Random said at length, pushing back his chair. "And some good has come out of all the trouble and bloodshed. Villareal's dream, his real dream, is coming true at last."

Gonzalez nodded. "When you told us how the *nativos* had joined together in 1855 to secure ownership of these lands—our lands—we realized it could be done. Even most of the hotheads were willing to listen." He looked at Roberto. "Of course, some heads are no longer so hot."

"I was a fool to ride with the *gorras*," Roberto said. "I believed it would help our people. I was wrong."

"True enough," Random agreed. "But that's done. I'm sure Señor Gonzalez will make an excellent president of your new association. As well as an excellent—how do you say it in Spanish? *Suegro.* An excellent father-in-law."

He stood. Joselito brought him coat and hat. "I must be on my way," he said. "Thank you for the meal. It was marvelous, as always."

Elena stood up and walked to his side. He took her hand and kissed it, smiling. "You will come to the wedding?" she asked.

"I may. I was planning to head for the Arizona Territory, but I may be back in the fall."

"You've never seen a Mexican wedding, have you *amigo?*" Eulógio Gonzalez asked. His black eyes sparkled.

"Not yet." Random took Gonzalez' hand and shook it.

"You claim that Elena squared my debt with you, by saving your life when my . . . my future son-in-law wanted to kill you. But I believe we owe you a greater debt than we can ever repay."

Random smiled. He smoothed his long hair back out of his eyes. "As a matter of fact," he said, "I was about to go over to the Anglo town to see about that very matter. Nine hundred fifty dollars is the debt *they* owe me. Elena, I wish you and Roberto every happiness." He started for the door.

"Señor Random?" It was Roberto.

Random looked back. *"Buena suerte,"* the boy said. "Good luck, you *gringo* bastard."

Random's militiamen had gone back to their homes. The single room of the frame schoolhouse seemed deserted. "You did the job for us, Mr. Random," Henry Bacon was saying, looking more solemn than ever. "It sure as hell didn't work out the way we figgered, though."

Tanner cleared his throat. "We got one more bit of business to tend to, afore you go," he said. "Doctor?"

Gravely, the doctor produced a thick envelope. He opened it and counted one thousand dollars in greenbacks onto the oaken desktop. "Payment agreed on in advance for services rendered," he said. "And fifty dollars' compensation for expenses incurred in performance of your job."

"Thank you very much." Random tucked the wad of bills into a pocket of his blue *capote*.

"Ahhh—this has been somewhat of an education for us all. And something of an embarrassment as well. Please accept our apologies. Our credulity almost cost you your life."

"It's nothing. Barnes took me in as well." He pulled out his watch. "I've got to be on my way, gentlemen. I want to get as far as I can before the light fails."

She was waiting for him outside the door of the schoolhouse. *How lovely she is in black,* he thought. "Good afternoon, Miss Barnes," he said.

"Good afternoon, Mr. Random," the girl replied, dropping her eyes. "I—I wanted to say I was sorry for the things I said. Back the other night. I didn't know—I didn't realize what was going on. My own Uncle Clay! I just can't imagine—"

"Then don't try. It won't do any good."

They stood facing each other in silence. Junella raised her face and looked at him. A tear left a glistening trail down her cheek. Then she gave a sob and threw her arms around him.

He held her, patting her till the crying eased. When she'd regained control she stepped back, straightening her veil.

"I cannot be as grateful to you as I know I should be," she said. "You—you killed him, after all. He was all the family I had left, even if he did . . . go bad."

"I understand."

"All I can say is, I'm terribly sorry."

"I am too," Random said. He looked her over again. She really was very beautiful. It was a pity things had to end this way. "Sorrier than you can know."

She held a gloved hand out for him to kiss, then turned and ran, back to the emptiness and memories in the great white mansion across the San Rael Trail.

When he was in the saddle he looked back to see someone standing on the steps of the school. "Mr. Carroll," he nodded.

"I was wrong about you, boy," the paunchy

rancher told him. "That's not an easy thing for a man like me to say. And I want you to know, from now on—you can just call me Tag." He stood there, beaming magnanimously all over his red face, thumbs hooked into the armholes of his vest.

The young man regarded him in silence for a moment. Then he laughed and spurred his horse off down the San Rael Trail.

EPILOGUE

Hoofbeats on the trail behind made Random turn in his saddle. When he saw who was following, he stopped the mare, letting her crop the black grama grass by the roadside.

"Mr. Random!" Sheriff Hoopwright called. His face was almost as red as Carroll's as he drew up beside the younger man.

"I missed you back at the schoolhouse," Random told him.

"Wanted to talk to you privatelike," Hoopwright said. His broken-down gelding was blowing hard. The sheriff of San Rael looked up and down the Trail, his Adam's apple going up and down like a cork floating on a fishing stream.

"What's on your mind, Sheriff?"

The sheriff glanced around again. "Well," he said. "I got Jerry Moody and them two cowhands of Clay's back at the jail."

"What about Slim Mason?" Random asked.

"He's alive," the sheriff said, "but just barely. Ain't woke up yet. When he does, Doctor says he don't think ol' Slim'll ever be quite right in the head again. I was thinking of puttin' him to work, sweepin' up round the jailhouse."

Random nodded. He had meant to kill the rasping, arrogant Mex-hater, but if this was the way it turned out, so be it. Raymond N. Mason, Slim to his friends, would never again scheme schemes, lay murderous ambushes, or try to end the lives of better

men than he at the end of a rope in a lonely byway.
"And the others?"

"That's what I wanted t'talk to you about. Cain't
hold 'em—ain't no evidence against 'em for nothing
but assault, and you won't press charges."

Random thought he knew where the weak-chinned
sheriff was leading. "So?"

For a third time Hoopwright scanned the Trail, as
if expecting a horde of Indians to pour out of the
woods and seize them. "Now, them boys are sure the
type to hold grudges, Mr. Random. And, hell, you
busted 'em up pretty good. The one you stuck in the
throat cain't talk louder'n a whisper, and sounds like
a rusty axle when he tries." His skinny fingers toyed
at his collar, and his tarnished silver badge. "They're
the kind who might, you know, try to track a body
down, even up the score a little bit."

"You want to give me a chance to kill them, is that
it?"

Hoopwright looked still more uncomfortable.

Random threw back his head and laughed. Hoopwright sat there on his gelding and squirmed. "If they
want to try to settle accounts with me," Random said,
"they are more than welcome to try." Hoopwright's
face fell. Random laughed again.

"It's about Freddie, isn't it? You wanted to trade
their lives for that treacherous whelp of a nephew.
Provided he's still alive." Hoopwright nodded,
stricken. His skin had turned slightly green.

"You needn't have worried," Random said heartily.
"I don't have him. You'd have found him soon
enough. Look in the back of that rank old warehouse
your office is in. He isn't damaged, not permanently.
The red paint and feathers ought to come off with
spirits of turpentine. I would have used tar instead of
paint, but McMurphey didn't have any in stock."

Hoopwright was gazing at him in horror. "What's
the matter?" Random asked. "He asked for it. Don't
look so shocked—I could have done for him the way

the Tuareg treat paid traitors. I told him about that, and he turned white as snow—under the paint and feathers, of course."

"Wh—what do the Tuaregs do?" Hoopwright inquired timidly.

Random told him. He turned white as snow.

The young man left him there with no more in the way of a farewell. Sheriff Hoopwright sat on his nag gazing after Random till his dust had long settled. Hoopwright's last view of him before he disappeared around a bend was of his long coattails trailing behind him, floating on the breeze like the final mocking laugh the sheriff thought he'd heard.

Dell Bestsellers

DELL'S
ACTION-PACKED
WESTERNS
Selected Titles

Comes the Blind Fury

John Saul

Bestselling author of
Cry for the Strangers
and *Suffer the Children*

More than a century ago, a gentle, blind child walked the paths of Paradise Point. Then other children came, teasing and taunting her until she lost her footing on the cliff and plunged into the drowning sea.

Now, 12-year-old Michelle and her family have come to live in that same house—to escape the city pressures, to have a better life.

But the sins of the past do not die. They reach out to embrace the living. Dreams will become nightmares.

Serenity will become terror. There will be no escape.

A Dell Book $2.75 (11428-4)

At your local bookstore or use this handy coupon for ordering: